"It's okay to only want sex,"

Rafe said, bringing her hands down against his thigh. Feeling Mackinley's fingers so near his zipper, Rafe shuddered, and he was rewarded with hearing another of her shaky breaths. Lifting his free hand, he cupped her chin. "I figure you got hurt real bad by your ex."

Mackinley nodded. "That's one way of putting it."

But in her marriage, Rafe guessed, she'd discovered she had needs that still wanted satisfaction. "There's no need for you to be alone. You can find a willing partner."

She licked her dry lips. "You think so, Rafe?"

"I know," he promised, pressing his lips to hers again. "Just kissing you makes me so hot," he whispered hoarsely, dragging his fingertips over her ribs again, touching a breast. They both gasped as he used a thumb to circle a tight nipple, and he loved how her breath started coming fast and labored. "It feels good, doesn't it?"

"Yes," she answered shakily. "It most certainly does."

Suddenly he bent and bit at her lower lip with sweet, savage hunger. Soon he was going to taste every inch of Mackinley Leigh. Soon he was going to give her everything she'd been missing. Soon...

Just as soon as he figured out what the hell she wanted from him....

Dear Reader,

Over the past few years, I've felt privileged to write
for many Harlequin series, including American
Romance, Intrigue and Love & Laughter, but
Temptation's new BACHELORS & BABIES
miniseries seemed the perfect opportunity to delve
into the kind of story I like best. To me, Temptation
has always offered readers the finest blend of humor
and intrigue, sensuality and action, so I hope you'll
enjoy *A Baby for the Boss,* in which a hotshot
hostage negotiator sets out to negotiate the release
of an ex-husband—only to have the tables turned,
and his own heart captured by a mother and child.

Do enjoy!

Best wishes,

Jule McBride

Books by Jule McBride

HARLEQUIN AMERICAN ROMANCE
658—COLE IN MY STOCKING
693—MISSION: MOTHERHOOD
725—DIAGNOSIS: DADDY
733—AKA: MARRIAGE
753—SMOOCHIN' SANTA
757—SANTA SLEPT OVER

A BABY FOR THE BOSS
Jule McBride

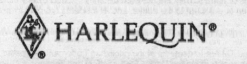

HARLEQUIN®

TORONTO • NEW YORK • LONDON
AMSTERDAM • PARIS • SYDNEY • HAMBURG
STOCKHOLM • ATHENS • TOKYO • MILAN • MADRID
PRAGUE • WARSAW • BUDAPEST • AUCKLAND

For Malle and Birgit—thanks!

ISBN 0-373-25861-5

A BABY FOR THE BOSS

1

"WHATEVER THEY DID to your old man in that place," Shark whispered with concern, "it's made him go soft."

Rafe nodded. So true. After returning from a synergy workshop, Rafe's father had started promoting male bonding, and all the touchy-feely business was getting awkward for the hostage negotiators at Ransom High Risk Negotiations, including Rafe. Even Mackinley Leigh, the brownnosing assistant Jack Ransom had so kindly hired for his son, wasn't making Rafe as uncomfortable as his dad's new need to hug in public.

Rifling worried fingers through his thick black hair, Rafe took in his dad's massive bald head, powerful shoulders, scarred chiseled face and beady black eyes. In addition to having virtually no neck and being minus a pinkie, Rafe's dad had more facial scars than a tomcat. Didn't he realize promoting sensitivity could be detrimental in the shady world of the kidnap insurance industry?

Rafe glanced past Mackinley to where wintery rays of five o'clock February darkness slanted against the jagged glass and steel Manhattan skyline, then at the fifteen angry hostage negotiators who were seated around the agency's new conference table staring at Rafe with pleading eyes.

Jack smiled. "I'm hoping this new round table will remind us all to focus on personal sharing and honest communication!"

Rafe's best friend, Shark, draped a gaudy oversize suit jacket on the back of his chair, then wearily smoothed a palm over his slicked-back black hair. "Sir, with all due respect, sir, honest communication during hostage negotiations could get us killed."

"Negative," countered Rafe's father in a voice so rough he could have chewed glass for breakfast. "With this round table, we'll start seeing ourselves as all for one and one for all."

"No offense, Dad," Rafe emphasized, knowing it was his duty to speak for the other men, "but we're hostage negotiators, not Musketeers."

The steely-eyed, hard-bodied negotiators nodded agreement, while their female assistants who were seated behind them continued taking meeting notes. Rafe knew these guys didn't give a damn about love or honor. They just wanted to turn a fast buck.

Shark's world-weary eyes narrowed, begging Rafe to put a leash on his dad. He whispered, "Do something, Rafe."

"This too shall pass," Rafe whispered back.

Looking mortified, Shark mouthed, "When?"

Soon, Rafe hoped. But they'd still have to live with the consequences of synergy. Namely Mackinley Leigh. While every other assistant had been hired from the Francesca modeling agency and had talents that ran to nail polishing, gum chewing and saucy flirtation, Jack had taken it upon himself to hire Mackinley for Rafe while Rafe was in Bogotá negotiating the release of a kidnaped executive. When Rafe returned, he'd exploded. He had the right to hire his own assistants, and prior to Mackinley, they'd all been convivial fashion models stuck between jobs.

Sincere and dedicated by contrast, Mackinley was scribbling down his father's every word as if her life depended on it. She had brown, innocent eyes, a short cap of wavy honey-gold hair tucked around unusually small, shapely ears, and pale reddish freckles that splashed across an uptilted nose that Rafe preferred not to recognize as cute. She wasn't more than five foot two, which made Rafe feel like a giant, and yet she was well-proportioned in ways he kept trying not to notice; a chocolate brown cashmere sweater hugged surprisingly full breasts, and Mackinley looked so inviting there, so touchably swollen and heavy, that unwanted hot-blooded desire threatened to surface as Rafe's gaze climbed the tempting sloping curves. Beneath the sweater and bra, he could even see the outline of relaxed nipples, a view that made his own chest turn unaccountably tight. He was fighting it, but damn if the woman hadn't gotten to him.

Forcing himself to look away, Rafe thought how different Mackinley was from his last assistant, Cindi, who'd always worn low-cut peasant blouses with ruffled miniskirts, and who had seized upon these meetings as the perfect opportunity to file her long, usually red talons. Unlike Cindi, Mackinley would probably never encourage Rafe's flirtations. He sighed. It was too bad Cindi had landed a job on television modeling designer jeans; after that, Mackinley arrived. She had an ivy league degree, was fluent in Spanish, was divorced but not looking, and had a baby. She also bit, rather than filed, her fingernails. She caught his gaze and Rafe smiled.

Politely, Mackinley smiled back, primly tugged down the knee-length hem of a tan wool skirt, then diverted those soft, startled-looking brown eyes. As she continued taking notes, her crossed leg began to swing, and Rafe had to fight not to reach over and stop it. Somehow, her movement grated like chalk on a blackboard, or like getting home from a Chinese take-out restaurant and realizing you forgot chopsticks. Imagining his fingers closing over—and stopping the movement of—Mackinley's smooth-looking, perfectly rounded knee, Rafe experienced another quickly denied rush of excitement before focusing on his father again.

"We've still got changes to make around the office," Jack was saying. "The assistants are seated *behind* their bosses during these staff meetings. So men, scoot back and make room. Won't it be better if we all sit together?"

There was an uncomfortable stunned silence, then a few animal-like grunts. Since the agency's founding, only male operatives had sat at the table during meetings.

"Jack," Shark protested, sounding positively shaken, "we already agreed to the new dress code." Yesterday, at Mackinley's instigation, Jack had announced the men were to wear suits rather than jeans to work, since the women always dressed up. Rafe was none too happy about the change; right now his only tie was choking him.

"Jack," said an ex-international spy who still went

by the codename Silencer, "if assistants sit at the table, they'll disrupt us when they refill our coffee."

A sharpshooter named Magnum added, "Excellent point, Silencer."

Rafe barely heard. "Dad," he began, acting as spokesperson for the employees, "it's after five, and I think I speak for everybody when I say we'd like to hit the road."

"Yet another excellent point," encouraged Magnum.

"But before that," continued Rafe, "the men asked me to talk to you about growing the business. We're heavily invested in making Ransom High Risk the top kidnap insurance industry agency, and we're already insuring multinational CEOs, bankers and politicians..."

"So, why not offer kidnap insurance to other high rollers?" asked Shark, picking up the thread. "Celebrities and athletes."

"Shark's right," said Rafe. "So, I've called a meeting this week with an advertising agency, Dad. Our clientele's private, but kidnap insurance is the wave of the future. We can even provide negotiators to the uninsured."

Silencer sounded interested. "The uninsured?"

Rafe nodded. "We guarantee delivery of trained hostage negotiators anywhere in the world within twenty-four hours, and right now we've got the highest return rate of hostages in the business, but we could offer other services, such as lost wage benefits and psychiatric evaluations for victims."

"Psychiatric evaluations?" said Jack pointedly.

His dad was implying that *he*, Rafe, needed such an

evaluation, but Rafe kept his temper in check. Still, pursuing the issue was a lost cause. Jack was beaming at Mackinley. It was embarrassingly evident that Jack was trying to get her interested in Rafe.

"Dad," Rafe continued with a sigh, "Right now, the men are worried about the bottom line. Some of these guys have wives. Kids. Families."

"I don't have any kids," Shark said, trying to be helpful. "But I am definitely looking to buy a boat."

"I support three ex-wives," added Silencer. After a moment of serious contemplation, he added, "and a dog also."

Jack's grim, close-mouthed smile was a reminder that he could be a thoroughly lethal character when not under the influence of synergy. "You guys get two thousand bucks a day for your services," he suddenly snarled. "You're not exactly *hurting* financially." Looking frustrated, he placed chunky elbows on the table and steepled beefy fingertips. "Am I still president of this agency?"

Rafe braced himself for his father's "My way or the highway" lecture. While Rafe was equally responsible for the creation of the business, his cantankerous dad held the superior title. "Sure, Dad, but..."

"Well, then." Jack smacked his fleshy lips with a tone of finality. "Now, scoot back, so the ladies can join us at the table."

Shelving his aggravation, Rafe scooted, and a second later, felt Mackinley's swinging toe lift his trouser leg. Thoroughly mystified by the jolts of awareness zipping through him, Rafe watched her in annoyed stupefaction. Her short fingers were always in motion, and for a second they lingered, a bitten-down nail anxiously fiddling with a gold, triangular earring.

"Mr. Ransom," she said in a husky voice that always took Rafe by surprise, since she definitely didn't look like the hoarse-voiced type.

Jack smiled. "Yes, Mackinley?"

"Thanks. It'll be so much easier to write on the table."

Rafe shot her a critical, sideways glance. "C'mon, it's not as if some caveman boss forces you to chisel meeting minutes on stone tablets."

Mackinley chuckled airily. "Oh, Rafe. You're so hard on yourself. You say that as if *you're* a caveman, as if you might actually drag a woman off by her hair!"

She was sorely tempting him. Rafe's eyes narrowed. On the surface, what she said sounded complimentary, which is how Jack would choose to interpret it, but her bemused tone implied Rafe lacked aggressive male qualities.

"Mackinley, do you really think Rafe's too hard on himself?" Jack asked, looking faintly pleased. "If so, it could be a sign of low self-esteem."

Rafe groaned. Around the table, men who'd seen too much of the world rolled shadowy eyes. "Dad," Rafe interjected before Mackinley could respond, "the men and I are glad you had that...that..."

"Sensitivity-building experience?" Mackinley supplied.

Rafe bristled, since the last thing he wanted was Mackinley's help in finishing his sentences. "Dad," he continued, keeping his tone even, "I speak for us all when I say we hope the synergy experience continues to enrich your life, but the market's tough. And we're dealing with kidnappers. We're not here to make friends, we're here to lock those guys away."

"A-men." Shark righteously straightened his broad, slouching shoulders.

Rafe tried to ignore his father's hurt expression, but when Jack frowned, myriad facial scars tugged downward, making him look strangely vulnerable even for an ex-hired gun.

"Bear with me, son," Jack said, running stubby fingers over his bald head as he abruptly changed the subject. "I need to make another announcement having to do with Mackinley."

If Rafe heard her name one more time he was going to throw up his hands, grab a suitcase and simply head for the islands. He wondered if he was jealous, since Mackinley had strapped Jack around her pinkie, but he decided his feelings were justified. No one liked her. The men kept kindly suggesting Rafe fire her. Today, Shark was wearing the ugliest suit imaginable—in protest against the new dress code, Rafe assumed. Yes, the way she was encouraging Jack was setting everybody's teeth on edge.

"I have one more item on my agenda," Jack continued.

We're waiting with baited breath. The raise of an eyebrow was the closest thing Rafe could muster to encouragement.

"An associate of mine suggested we try an exercise that's worked wonders at his sugar refinery, and since so many of us are in New York—"

"We're usually on the road," Rafe interjected.

"Having this many guys in town means business is down, Dad."

"Sir, I'm getting an ulcer, sir," Shark put in.

"High blood pressure," added Silencer.

"Dad," Rafe continued, "these men want to make money."

"Money comes and goes," sighed Jack, "but the relationships we build today can last forever."

Silencer made a soft, choking sound.

Rafe shut his eyes. Waited. Opened them.

"No," Shark whispered. "You're not imagining this."

No, and if Mackinley Leigh wasn't here egging on his old man, these formidable, leery eyes that had stared down snipers, armed enemy soldiers and tanks wouldn't be shooting pleading glances toward Rafe. However, as Rafe's father began detailing the office exercise he had in mind, eyes that had seen so much of the world began to widen. Shark snickered, and Magnum's broad shoulders shook with barely concealed laughter while Rafe forced himself to remain calm.

"Team building!" Jack declared when he was finished. "It's a great idea, right Rafe? A real win-win. What have you got to say?"

Say? Rafe was speechless. When he realized his father was serious, panic seized him. "You want Mackinley and I to trade places?"

The corners of Jack's dark, foreboding eyes crinkled with pleasure. "Like I said, this exercise helped produce new win-win situations at my friend's sugar refinery."

"I think we're as refined as we need to be," Rafe said.

"As sweet, too," agreed Shark.

"If you ask me," added Silencer, "one-sided wins are fine. I'm okay with just a win, Jack. Not a win-win."

Magnum was starting to look puzzled. "Wait a minute," he said. "I don't get it. If two guys are competing, why would you want both of them to win? That wouldn't be fair, would it?"

Jack ignored Magnum and rushed on. "C'mon, Rafe. How many fathers can give their sons a real-life opportunity to walk in someone else's shoes?"

Thankfully not many. Sourly, Rafe glanced down at Mackinley's stocking-clad calf, to where a taupe, no-nonsense pump had disengaged from her heel and dangled from a toe. She had delicate feet, he couldn't help but notice. Small ankles. High arches.

"You'll walk in her shoes," his father was saying. "Trade cars, apartments..."

Rafe wondered how much paperwork was involved in having his father committed. At least Mackinley looked equally stunned. For once, Rafe guessed she wouldn't encourage Jack's lunacy. "You mean let her drive my Humvee?"

"A Humvee?" Now Mackinley sounded interested.

Jack smiled. "By next week, you'll understand how it feels to be the boss, Mackinley."

"How it feels? I'm sure Rafe has feelings," Mackinley murmured demurely.

"Oh, I have feelings," Rafe whispered, his eyes settling on the pale creamy column of her neck, which was ringed by a thin gold chain that disappeared inside her sweater and was of the sort that usually had ice skates or a tennis racket attached. "Right now I'm about to wring your neck."

She merely smiled, her eyes steadily holding his father's. "Mr. Ransom," she said, raising her voice, "I think yours is an absolutely lovely idea."

"Good. At the end of a week," Jack continued, "you'll both report to the group. This will be a real growth experience for us all. I wish *I* was trading places with Mackinley."

Rafe waited, knowing Mackinley would have to protest this once. But no. She didn't bother to intervene, and now Rafe could no longer hold back his annoyance. "I wish you were, too. What did they do to you in that place, Dad?"

"What place?" asked Jack innocently.

Rafe's voice lowered in warning. "You know what place." Big bad Jack had left for the synergy workshop a man, and he'd come back...emasculated. The men were appalled. And there was no way Mackinley Leigh was parking her beige-clad butt on Rafe's black leather sofa. Or drinking imported lagers from his fridge while she fiddled with the all-American phallic symbol—meaning his remote control. Nor was she sleeping alone between Rafe's black silk sheets. Visions of Mackinley's apartment came to Rafe's mind. He imagined a living room full of what would look like office furniture.

And a baby.

Relief flooded him. "She's got a baby. I can't have a baby in my place. Uh, it's...it's in the lease, Dad." That probably wasn't strictly true, but Rafe thought it sounded good. Besides, if there was one thing Manhattanites understood, it was the ever-present threat of losing their apartments.

For the first time, Mackinley's voice faltered. "Uh...Kimmie can stay home, and you can baby-sit, Rafe. And anyway, my mom lives with me."

Rafe gasped. "You think I'd stay with your *mother*?"

"Her mother!" Jack exclaimed in satisfied approval. "Next week, Rafe will report back, telling us what it's like to be a single parent."

"You know what it's like, Dad," Rafe reminded him, feeling ice curl through his veins. "You raised me by yourself." Pausing, Rafe considered the best possible negotiating angles, then continued. "I don't care who's around to help me with Mackinley's baby. No mother in her right mind leaves a baby with a man like me. Mackinley," Rafe added pragmatically, since she'd left him no choice but to call her bluff, "you're only pretending to go along with this because you know it'll never happen. I'm going to wind up talking Dad out of it, while you look flexible and accommodating, right?"

"I'm doing my job," she returned.

"And don't talk about me as if I'm not here, son."

Rafe shouldn't have. Countering Jack was always a bad move. The more resistance Jack felt, the more he pushed. With or without Synergy, Jack Ransom was a pit bull, and now Rafe had the sinking feeling that a lose-lose was imminent.

"Let me put it this way," Jack suddenly said. "If you don't do this son, you're fired."

"Now, that's team building at its finest," Rafe said dryly, knowing he'd allow no other man on earth to talk to him this way.

"Make your choice, son."

Shooting Mackinley a dark look, Rafe noticed her smile was now strangely, falsely bright. The room had gone dead silent. Didn't Mackinley understand Jack was serious? That Rafe's job was now on the line? Even Jack looked guilty, since he'd backed Rafe into a corner. Rafe sighed. He loved his father more than life, but at moments such as this he definitely didn't like him.

"You'd leave your *baby* with me, Mackinley?" Rafe asked silkily, settling his glowering green eyes on hers. Relieved to see doubt and concern clouding her expression, Rafe felt sure she'd come to her senses. "Dad's going to do this to us." Lowering his voice seductively as he often did when negotiating with female clients, he forged on, no longer caring that other negotiators were present, or that Jack's real motive was matchmaking, since Mackinley was so obviously the kind of girl Jack thought Rafe should marry. "C'mon," Rafe persuaded softly, "help me out."

She gulped nervously, but held her ground. "Really, I think it's great. Your dad's right. We'll learn so much."

Silencer didn't bother to muffle his chuckle. Shark hooted, and Rafe continued staring steadily at Mackinley, wondering at her possible motives. Jack's menacing eyes darted around the table. "Meeting's over. Rafe and I'll hash out the remaining details."

If there'd been a bomb threat, the room couldn't have cleared faster. After everyone was gone, Rafe turned to his dad, determined to talk some sense into him. "Think this through, Dad. I'm not worried about myself, of course," he said, flawlessly arguing his position, "but the last thing a sensible, divorced single parent such as Mackinley needs is a stranger moving in with her mother. And how will that poor, lonely little baby feel without its mommy?" Rafe winced, knowing he was stooping low for the sake of argument. "And what's Mackinley's *mom* going to say about this? She's an older lady, no doubt, and she won't want a strange man in her home, now will she? How would *you* feel, Dad, if I suddenly brought a stranger to stay with you? Someone you'd never even met before?"

Jack hung his head guiltily.

Good. Rafe had stuck in the knife, and now all he had to do was turn it. "Dad," he coaxed, "I know what you're trying to do, and I appreciate the gesture, I really do. You're trying to fix me up with Mackinley, but—"

"Mackinley's so nice," Jack interrupted petulantly, thrusting out his thick lower lip.

"She types sixty words a minute, I'll give you that," Rafe agreed reasonably. "And she's prompt."

"She's *attractive*."

Rafe grunted softly in exasperation as he and his father stood. "In her own special way," Rafe forced himself to concede, still bothered by how drawn he was to her. Damsels in distress were common as Mondays in this line of work, and because the type wreaked havoc with Rafe's emotions, he steered clear of them. Mackiney might not need Rafe's help at this particular moment, but she was so obviously trusting and gullible that someone would eventually notice and take advantage. Rafe didn't plan on being there when it happened.

Sighing, he glanced over his dad's short, beefy, battle-scarred frame. Where was the father he knew and loved, the macho man who always encouraged Rafe's amorous adventures? Years ago, after Rose Ransom had died, Jack left the military, became a mercenary and dragged Rafe all over the globe. Despite difficult circumstances, his dad had been a good parent, insisting Rafe attend college and join the army, both of which he felt would build Rafe's character. Some days, Rafe was pretty sure neither had. "Dad, don't make me do this."

"Rafe," his father said, "you're thirty-two now. I was ten years younger than you when I married Rose."

Rafe was only two when Rose died, and ever since, he and Jack had been a team, tough guys who got along fine without women in their lives. Briefly, Rafe recalled his last steady girlfriend, Charmaine—and wished he hadn't. *So much for women.* "Your point is?"

"I'm your father. I don't have to have a point."

Rafe thrust his fingers through his hair to relieve frustration. His hands landed on his hips. "I didn't understand why you hired Mackinley, but I do now. You're matchmaking, Dad, but don't dump your guilt on me."

Jack had far too many facial nicks and scars to look truly innocent. "Guilt?"

Dragging a motherless son all over the globe hadn't made for the best of childhoods, and now, just because he'd gone to a synergy workshop, Jack had decided to make amends by marrying Rafe off. It was really too much. For years, no living woman had ever stacked up to Rose, and Jack Ransom had played the field, encouraging Rafe to do the same. "C'mon, Dad, you always told me not to settle down."

Jack looked depressed. "What's *wrong* with Mackinley? She's respectable."

"Who wants *respectable?*" Suddenly Rafe bit out an embarrassed curse. "Mackinley, I didn't realize you were here."

She was haunting the conference room doorway like a ghost, color splotching her pale cheeks; the freckles scattered across her nose seemed to darken. "Obviously."

He winced. "Sorry." Well, at least she'd come to help with his father. One word from Mackinley, and Jack would back down. No such luck, Rafe realized a second later.

"Trading places is such a wonderful idea, Mr. Ransom," Mackinley began, "and I'm sure you've thought of everything, but I just wanted to double-check. We'll be getting overtime, since Rafe and I will be working nights?"

"I can't believe my oversight," Jack returned. "Absolutely. Overtime it is, Mackinley."

Talk about negotiating skills, Rafe thought as she squared her shoulders, turned and retreated without offering him so much as another glance. His mouth went bone dry. Ninety-nine times out of a hundred he went for tall, slender women whose eyes met his dead-on and who were straightforward about taking their pleasure, but Mackinley was the one-percent that argued for the hard-to-get girl next door. *Definitely respectable*, Rafe thought, his eyes trailing from the cashmere sweater, to the tan wool skirt, to the practical taupe pumps. A healthy pull of arousal was mixed with grudging respect. At least she'd gotten them overtime.

"I won't fire you," Jack said, taking lumbering steps toward Rafe. "Not if you trade places with Mackinley. And, trust me, son, you're going to thank me for this."

"Don't count on it. And I know you won't really fire me."

"I might."

Given his dad's unpredictable behavior since the synergy workshop, Rafe feared it was possible. Before he could respond, Jack lunged and threw his beefy arms around Rafe's waist. Gasping, Rafe braced himself as his barrel-like chest thudded against Jack's. "Dad," he protested.

"I didn't hug you enough as a child," moaned Jack.

Awkwardly, Rafe thumped his father's shoulder. "Please, Dad." He sighed. "You did fine."

"No," Jack ground out. "Nothing will be right until you're as happy as I was when I met Rose."

Rafe bit back a protest, and as soon as he could disengage himself, he stepped back and peered into his father's eyes. Dark and beady, they were hardened by years of military and mercenary life, and yet they were so misty Rafe knew there was no point in arguing further. His old man had lost it.

Heaving another sigh, Rafe excused himself and headed for Mackinley, who he found in the carpet-walled cubicle outside his office, her tush swaying as she switched off a computer. Turning, she settled her rump against the desk's edge. "I'm about ready to leave. Mom's picking Kimmie up at day care, so I can show you our place immediately, and you can give me the keys to yours."

Was she crazy? Rafe scrutinized her as he entered the cubicle. "We've only worked together two weeks and you hardly know me. Why would you agree to do this, Mackinley?"

"We don't have a choice." She edged unsuccessfully backward, stretching an arm behind her, her ever-nervous fingers toying with items on the desk—a pen, a pencil, a sheet of paper.

As a hostage negotiator, Rafe was used to second-guessing people, but after two weeks, he remained clueless concerning Mackinley's agenda. He simply couldn't get a handle on her. She seemed to be a do-gooder, a champion of the underdog and a people pleaser, but why would his father's opinion be that important to her? Why hadn't she told Jack not to interfere in her personal life?

Rafe wasn't proud of it, but he was running out of tactics for intimidating Mackinley, so he used the age-old male trick of physical proximity, coming closer and hoping the nearness of his gym-hardened body might startle her into changing her mind. Instead the movement affected *him*, sending his pulse racing. His voice turned husky. "We can't trade places," he ventured softly. "I have a *life*."

Her intriguing brown eyes suddenly blazed with determination he couldn't understand. "I don't?"

"Of course you do. Doesn't your baby need you at home?"

At that, she looked worried, and Rafe tried to tell himself he was noticing her eyes because of their frightened expression, not because the irises were such an alluring, sexy, velvet brown. "We have no choice, Rafe," she repeated, her voice now sounding as low and persuasive as his. "You don't want to lose your job, now do you?"

"Damn if I do," Rafe admitted, fighting his reaction to her voice. Women like her, he decided, shouldn't have voices like that. Hers was dangerously throaty, just shy of rough, and even though Rafe figured she never tossed back shots of whiskey or smoked cigarettes, her voice reminded him of sultry lounge acts and dark, smoky bars. Tilting his head, he gazed down, then frowned. He was accustomed to subterfuge, to staring into lying eyes, but he was surprised to realize Mackinley Leigh was hiding something. Surely he was wrong, he told himself, but he was half tempted to trade places, just to sneak a peek at her lifestyle. Gazing deeply into her eyes, he decided he was being distrustful without cause; it was an occupational hazzard.

"Your dad really might fire you," Mackinley pressed.

Fighting frustration by taking a deep breath, Rafe tried to ignore how the scent of her came with it. "You're trading places with me because you're concerned about my welfare?"

"You're totally misunderstanding me, Rafe. I don't *want* to do this. It's our *job*."

"Are you doing it for the overtime pay?" he suddenly guessed.

She nodded. "Yes...yes, that's it. I need the money."

He couldn't ignore the onslaught of guilt. Assistants weren't paid much, and maybe she needed money for the baby. Feeling strangely protective, Rafe reached without thinking and touched her shoulder, the soft cashmere sweater seeming to melt under the heat of his fingertips.

Her eyes widened. "Rafe?"

He didn't answer. He pressed his lower body so close that their thighs brushed for the briefest second, and the contact stole his breath. His voice turned coarse as sandpaper. "If it's money you need, Mackinley, I'll write you a check in the amount of the overtime pay." Vaguely, he wondered what he was doing. He knew better than to get involved with soft-looking women who would probably wind up needing his protection for one reason or another. "Just come and help me talk my dad out of this."

"You think you can buy me off? Just like that?"

Why was she protesting? "You said you need money. I'm trying to help." Damn if those trusting eyes of hers weren't already tying Rafe in knots. No, he definitely couldn't get involved, much less stay with her mother and baby. He stared at the giggling, photogenic baby in the Plexiglas cube on her desk, then his eyes returned to her, tracing the almost girlish features and golden pixie haircut. Right now, the fluorescent lights made it seem as if a halo had settled on the fine strands. They looked more gold than honey-colored at the moment, and his muscles clenched in reaction, reminding him to get away from her. "C'mon, Mackinley," he coaxed. "Why not just take the money?"

She didn't answer, and during the pause he realized she couldn't be more than twenty-five, which meant too young for him. Against all common sense, he suddenly murmured, "I make you nervous, don't I?"

She eyed him. "A little."

"Well, you've bothered me ever since I laid eyes on you, too." He felt the unsufferable truth of it in the rigidness of thighs that were straining toward hers, and in the sudden wrenching throb of his groin.

She looked surprised. "I bother you?"

More than you'll ever know. "You're too interested in this job," Rafe returned, wishing he wasn't so thoroughly aware of her body, of how warm it felt by contrast to the cold, darkening night beyond the office windows. "With your language skills, you could make more money as a translator." She could have worked for a publishing house or the U.N. Her skills were valuable here, but not necessary. "I want to know why you're indulging my old man's every whim."

Her anxious hands had been flitting over the desk. With their short, bitten nails, they shouldn't have been interesting to watch, but they were. Surprisingly, she lifted one, resting her fingertips on his suit lapel, and the movement pushed ripples into his bloodstream. "I didn't mean to bother you, Rafe."

Then stop. "If you're trying to stop me from advancing, you probably can't," he warned, a smile touching his lips as he glanced down to where her fingertips connected with his chest. Without thinking, he readjusted his stance so that his thigh further pressured the yielding softness of hers. Damn if she wasn't supposed to shriek sexual harassment, or turn in her resignation, but Rafe was glad she didn't. "If I didn't know better," he found himself teasing, trying his best to appear unaffected, "I might think you're actually encouraging me."

"I'm indulging your *dad* because he's the boss."

"Is that so?" Slowly, Rafe's thumb rubbed a circle on her cashmere-clad shoulder, and when she still didn't run screaming to daddy, he said, "I'm the boss, too, Mackinley."

"Meaning?"

"Want to indulge my whims?"

Her head was tilted upward and he could see the pulse in her throat ticking rapidly; the freckles sprinkled across her nose seemed to deepen in color. "You'd like that, wouldn't you, Rafe?"

"Couldn't say until you let me taste a sample."

She nervously tossed her short, golden hair, and he liked how she did it, as if she possessed the mane of a lioness instead of inches-long hair that barely curled around her ears. He fought the urge to trace a finger around one of the silken-looking waves. "Don't forget this was your father's idea," she said, her breath catching, her voice deepening. "It's not as if I want a stranger sleeping in my bed, you know."

He watched, riveted, as the pink spear of her tongue flicked out anxiously to lick her lower lip, and something fluttery took flight inside his chest. "A stranger? Or me?"

Those heart-stirring, trusting brown eyes hardened into a glare, but it was hardly menacing. "You. Believe it or not, you're not *my* type either, Rafe."

Lowering his head, he scrutinized her, their thighs more than brushing now, his green eyes gentling. "But wouldn't attraction to me explain your constant prickliness, and your willingness to go through with this scheme of my dad's?"

She gaped at him. "You're crazy."

He merely smiled. "Maybe it would account for

why you're tolerating our physical contact right now." Pressing his thumb harder into the delicate hollow where her shoulder and collarbone met, he rubbed a deeper, more intimate, caressing circle. His voice was pure silk. "You're attracted to me, aren't you?"

She sized him up for a long moment, and when she spoke, her words were barely audible. "Maybe I'm trying to decide."

"I think you already have. I know I've formulated a theory."

"You have?"

Rafe nodded. "You're divorced," he said. "Not ready for anything serious, and maybe wanting a little male companionship, preferably with a free-and-easy type of man who would never break your heart." Maybe she was even thinking her mother could watch the baby tonight, so they could go to his place.

"Sounds like you're considering working on more than your sensitivity this week," Mackinley returned dryly.

He chuckled easily. "It could be a win-win."

She rolled her eyes. "For whom?"

He laughed. "So, you really don't want to sleep in my bed?" he prodded with another quick smile, this one nothing more than a flash of straight white teeth.

Her voice lacked conviction. "Nope."

"Yet," Rafe countered huskily, his hand flexing around her shoulder, finding surprising strength there in the toned muscles beneath the cashmere. "Don't you mean you're not ready to sleep in my bed *yet*, Mackinley?"

"I'd need some convincing," she murmured.

"My pleasure," he whispered. He drew her nearer and simply, shamefully crushed his hot, expert lips down on hers in a kiss that promised the sweetest of dark temptations.

2

WE'LL FINISH THIS later, Mackinley.

When his father appeared, Rafe had broken their kiss with that husky promise, leaving Mackinley feeling strangely hollow and swollen inside, so knock-kneed, shaky and unbalanced that she'd barely been able to follow Mr. Ransom downstairs, where he'd supervised her and Rafe's exchange of car keys.

Now Rafe was following her home, and she was overwrought because his tanklike Humvee was so much like him—solid, massive and impossible to maneuver. Nevertheless, she was in dire straits, so the Humvee might come in handy; it offered more protection than her silver compact, just in case things turned nasty. Nastier, Mackinley mentally corrected as she sucked in a quavering breath and glanced into the rearview mirror.

"Rafe," she murmured simply, seeing him behind her. Anxiously, she lifted a hand from the steering wheel and chewed her thumbnail. As much as she needed him, she'd learned one thing during her two-week tenure at Ransom High Risk: Rafe hated helpless women, and he'd probably only help one with whom he was sleeping.

Which meant Mackinley had to seduce him. Her husband had convinced her that starching his shirts was her strong suit, not sex, but luckily Rafe was a breathtaking specimen of a man. That would help. Merely seeing him scrunched in her tiny car set her already jittery nerves further on edge. He was uncommonly big—humongous really—with a football player's broad shoulders that were stretching a black overcoat he never bothered to button, biceps that bulged under his shirt sleeves, and hard thighs that bunched under his slacks. During their kiss, he'd strained against every inch of trouser fabric, especially where it was naughtiest to notice—and that fact was still jangling Mackinley's every last nerve.

Not that she had any choice but to seduce him. She'd have to do it, even if he was ugly. But, of course Rafe wasn't ugly. Far from it.

Her heart palpitating, Mackinley darted her eyes to the rearview mirror again and the mouth he'd settled so wolfishly over hers. It was bracketed by two deep grooves, and his lips were full and sensual, redder than any man's had a right to be. His pelt of thick jet hair had felt soothingly silken against her cheek, and she could still feel the faintly abrasive, exciting burn of his rough stubbly jaw. Black eyebrows and a fringe of inky eyelashes framed smoky green eyes that always smouldered with intent.

Even his hands excited her. Curled tightly over the steering wheel of her little car, they were thick-fingered and strong, almost beefy. Despite the rein of terror under which she was living—the real reason she'd taken the job at Ransom High Risk—she couldn't keep her eyes off his hands. If hands really indicated the southward contours of a man, a woman would be in very serious trouble with Rafe.

She was going to be in trouble.

Suppressing a shiver, Mackinley stared again through the windshield into the early evening darkness. Bright red greeting cards, heart-shaped candy boxes and bouquets of flowers were displayed in the storefronts along Broadway, reminding her it was Valentine's Day. Her heart aching, she realized how much she missed the normalcy of sharing a simple romantic dinner with a man who loved her.

Rafe, that definitely wasn't.

But according to her research, he was the best hostage negotiator in New York City, which was why she'd gone to Ransom High Risk to fling herself on his mercy. Instead, she'd been mistaken for a job applicant interested in the position Cindi had vacated. Determined to turn things to her advantage when she realized Rafe would be her boss, Mackinley had interviewed with Jack, then waited for Rafe's return. According to one news article, Rafe had once gone five days without sleep while negotiating the release of twenty-four kindergarten kids from a hijacked bus. Because Rafe was so dedicated, Mackinley had every reason to hope he might have a soft spot and take pity on her. Even now, because of how well he'd handled those kids, she had no qualms about leaving him with Kimmie. No baby could be safer.

Not that Rafe was going to take pity.

When he'd returned to New York, he'd taken one glittery, green-eyed look at Mackinley, then stormed into his father's office and slammed the door. The shouting match lasted a half hour.

Ever since, Mackinley had been devising ways to butter him up. Four times she'd approached him with hypothetical charity cases—only to finally have him roar, "Don't kid yourself, sweetheart. I'm not going to risk getting shot for free. Who told you that Ransom High Risk is a not-for-profit organization? Does this look like Save the Whales? The Animal Rescue League? The Rafe Ransom *Foundation?*"

At that moment, Mackinley had come close to hating him.

Jack Ransom wouldn't help. Despite all he'd learned in his synergy workshop—something the man sorely needed—Jack still had a hair-trigger temper, and since he thought Mackinley was the best thing since sliced bread, he'd only feel betrayed if he ever realized she'd come to Ransom High Risk with a hidden agenda. As much as she needed help, she hated ruining his high opinion of her. Besides, Jack had begun clumsily matchmaking, which was why she and Rafe were trading places. Everyday, Jack hovered around Mackinley's cubicle, offering mournful monologues about Rafe's motherless childhood, assuring Mackinley that Rafe's rough ways could be tempered only by a sweet woman like herself.

"Sweet?" she whispered nervously, hating to disappoint Jack. Reaching to the passenger seat, she patted a canvas handbag, feeling the gun inside. Right now, danger was everywhere.

Especially behind her.

Well, hopefully tonight wouldn't be her only chance to seduce Rafe. She needed time alone in his apartment first, since he was working on a home database containing names of professional kidnappers and stool pigeons. Tonight she'd print what she could. She just wished she could afford Rafe's exorbitant fee of two thousand dollars a day, but she couldn't. When it came to hostage negotiators, pricing was definitely exclusionary. She suddenly swallowed around the dryness of her throat, thinking that seducing Rafe into helping her might not be so...terrible.

Suddenly, the phone rang.

Gasping, fighting down an all-too-familiar surge of panic, she tightened a trembling hand on the steering wheel, reached for the passenger seat, fumbled in her handbag for the phone, flipped it open and shoved it between her jaw and the shoulder Rafe had caressed just moments ago. She damned her voice for shaking as she spoke. "Hello?"

No one answered. She suspected the call came from a phone booth somewhere in Manhattan and her panicked eyes darted around the crowded street as she strained, trying to hear over the traffic sounds, hoping for a clue as to the location of the caller. "I know you're there," she began, "so...please, please talk to me."

Why couldn't people stop shouting and blowing their horns? "I'm listening. I'm here. I'll do anything you want."

Not that she really could, she thought, the blood freezing in her veins, running as cold as ice. Didn't the caller know she was out of money? That she was emotionally overwrought, her carefully guarded facade close to crumbling? Had they guessed she'd finally gone to Ransom High Risk? Were they watching her?

Terrified, she glanced in the rearview mirror. Behind her, city lights brightened the compact's interior, and somehow, seeing the determined, rigid set of Rafe's dark, whiskered jaw, and the direct, intense expression of his eyes provided strange, unexpected comfort.

A garbled voice said, "You got the forty thousand?"

"Yes."

"You'll get instructions. Follow them, or we kill him."

The phone went dead.

They'd call back. They always did. Or worse, maybe they wouldn't. That was Mackinley's deepest fear. One day, maybe the phone that was never beyond her reach would simply quit ringing.

And she'd never know if Kimmie's daddy was dead.

Stuffing down heart-pounding panic, she gritted her teeth determinedly. Countless times, when he was alive, her daddy had said the Leighs were too proud to air dirty laundry, but at this point she'd pasted a smile on her face when she was dying inside for so long that she didn't think she could stand it anymore. It helped that her dad would have been proud of her though; she'd held on this long for her mom and Kimmie, and she could continue to do so.

I've got to seduce Rafe into helping me soon.

She could smile while she did it, too. Already, something about him, maybe his sheer brute strength, had allowed her to breathe easier. It shouldn't have happened, but she trusted him enough to let go of her fear because she knew he was the one man who could help. Unexpectedly, moments ago, the heat of his hard, uncompromising mouth and powerful body had made her forget the ordeal entirely. She'd melted, the slow thrusting slide of his tongue touching the very core of her while his massively strong arms offered safe harbor. Remembering the kiss, she felt flustered. Rafe had been obviously stunned by her compliance, but for a lost rapturous moment, he seemed to be everything she'd fantasized—a knight in shining armor.

She was desperate for one.

Realizing she was still clutching the phone, she quickly called her mother to explain why she was bringing Rafe home, then she replaced the phone in her handbag, next to the gun. She withdrew a mentholated cough drop—they kept her from biting her nails, however temporarily—and her hand trembled as she unwrapped it and popped it into her mouth.

Behind her, the object of her seduction attempt was still dwarfed in the compact, uncomfortably crouched over the wheel. No matter how far Rafe pushed back the seat, Mackinley knew his long legs wouldn't have room.

Shuddering, she remembered the feel of them, how heat poured from the braced-apart, rigid, hard-bunched thighs, and from the unmistakable mound beneath his fly. Her heart hammered with the danger of what she'd felt there. Heat flooded her cheeks, flushing her with excitement she couldn't believe she was capable of feeling right now, but no one—not even her husband, Oliver—had ever kissed her with such demanding force. And while Rafe had meant to scare her out of trading places for the week, he'd only made her anticipate the previously unwanted task of seduction that lay ahead.

She gritted her teeth. She could do it. She knew she wasn't Rafe's type—he always hired leggy women from the Francesca modeling agency and Shark said

Rafe's ex-girlfriend was a jazz singer. Still, given his response to her, Rafe might still be receptive to the other things Mackinley so desperately needed from him.

RAFE WAS SURPRISED by Mackinley's tumbledown apartment building. He set the garment bag he kept at the office in case he had to go to the airport on short notice near the lobby door and simply looked around. "You live here?"

"Home sweet home."

Barely visible in the dark lobby, Mackinley leaned against a painted, flaking metal stair rail in such a lazy wanton way that only her conservative camel coat and neat, trim outfit kept her from looking like the proverbial streetwalker. Seeing the blatant manner in which she was sizing him up, Rafe smiled. He was used to female attention, perfectly comfortable with his own sexuality, and glad Mackinley was warming to him. "I don't know about you," he said with a soft chuckle as he approached her, "but after that kiss at the office, I don't want to stop now."

She casually unbuttoned her coat. "Who says you have to?"

"No one, apparently." Pushing back the open sides of his coat, he simply, unapologetically locked his hips to hers, feeling pulsing jolts of heat course between them. She was small, irresistibly feminine, and as his big hands curled around a surprisingly tiny waist, almost circling it, the feminine warmth of chocolate cashmere teased his palms. Amazing. Just touching Mackinley made the evident, almost painful arousal he'd fought so hard to hide at the office return.

Even more amazing, she didn't seem to mind.

Rafe gazed down at her, aching, and judging from her dark, flashing, narrow-eyed gaze, she was feeling exactly the same. It was definitely the wrong time to get a stab of conscience. "But we work together," he reminded her. "Kisses are one thing, but we seemed to be heading for a bedroom."

She laughed softly. "You sound hopeful."

"Maybe I am."

She eyed him curiously. "Anyway, you started this, Rafe."

"Want to finish it, too. But maybe it's not wise."

"Your assistants never last long," she commented silkily.

"What? Are you quitting?" Even as he said the words, Rafe realized he no longer wanted her to. His assistants usually got modeling jobs, though, and with her education and language fluency, Mackinley would eventually find other work.

"Someday," she said reasonably, resting her palm on the lapel of his coat. "So maybe we shouldn't worry about our relationship as co-workers. Besides, your dad wants us to...spend time together."

Rafe sighed in exasperation. "My father thinks we should get married, Mackinley."

Another smile curled the corners of her mouth. "I like your dad."

That fact, like her husky voice, made Rafe feel better than it should have. "Me, too," he mused. "Not everyone warms to Jack, you know. Most women are too put off by his appearance to get to know him."

Mackinley's low, soft chuckle was seductive, lingering on the cool air like music. "The jagged scar on his left cheek can be off-putting," she agreed. "But your dad's sincere. I think he'd help any friend in trouble."

"He's definitely taken a shine to you." And standing in the foyer, tightening his hands on her tiny waist, Rafe admitted he had, too. Nevertheless, despite Mackinley's and his dad's green lights, Rafe forced himself to glance around, sensing something about the setup wasn't right. "Not the kind of place where I thought you'd live," he said, not letting the dank surroundings stop him from enjoying her body heat as he changed the subject.

She sounded defensive. "What did you expect?"

He lifted his broad shoulders in a shrug. "Some place fancier." Maybe something near Central Park where he lived. Assistants at Ransom weren't well paid, but given her education, general bearing and closetful of cashmere, Rafe wouldn't have been surprised to find that she had a trust fund, or a hefty settlement from her divorce. His eyes swept from the brown silk scarf circling her milky neck down the length of her coat. He guessed the clothing labels were from good stores.

"Upstairs isn't bad," she assured him, her persuasive voice throaty. "You'll be comfortable here, Rafe."

Not as comfortable as he'd be at home. Despite the freshly painted walls and recently mopped floors, the brick walk-up felt damp and had dim overhead lights and plumbing Rafe could hear in the walls. That she lived here just didn't seem right. Neither did the fact that she parked so far from the office when employee parking was available, or that she drove at all, since the subway would be faster.

"Don't mean to be rude," Rafe said. "It's just not

what I expected." A slow smile formed. "And you're not, either."

"Meaning?"

He eyed her a long moment. He'd known better than to kiss such an innocent-looking, trusting woman, but now there was no turning back. After a taste of Mackinley, he couldn't stop if he wanted to. He'd discovered a mixture of uncertainty and eagerness that was driving him wild. He summed it up by saying, "I think I'm starting to like you, Mackinley."

"Over the past couple of weeks, I've gotten to know you, Rafe. And think I like you, too."

His eyes narrowed with suspicion. "Hard to believe I've done anything to make you like me."

"You were mad because your dad hired me without consulting you," she said graciously. "It's perfectly understandable. You weren't predisposed to like me."

"Well, I do now." His gaze dropping to her lips, he took in the smear of pink glossy lipstick and recalled how easily she'd opened her mouth for him, and how the soft slow sexy pull of her tongue had felt suckling his. He lifted a hand and swept his knuckles against her satiny cheek, finding it still cool from the February evening and as silken as her scarf. "On the way over, do you know what I was thinking about?" She shook her head, and he noted the slight flush rising on her winter-pale skin and the flutter of anticipation visible in the pulse at her throat. He smiled. "I think you do."

Her brown eyes sparkled. "Too bad I'm not your type."

Damn if Mackinley Leigh wasn't a class-A flirt, too. And Rafe just loved a woman with strong verbal skills. "You know my type?"

"I've done research."

"Then put this in your dictionary, sweetheart." Angling his head down, he quickly, wetly kissed the smirk off her mouth. He felt it vanish beneath his lips, leaving what felt like a softer smile. A cough drop she'd been sucking was almost gone, and as he licked the remaining sliver from her tongue, the hot-cold mint taste of menthol hit him, making his shoulders prickle with a cold sweat. Playfully, he pushed the drop back into her mouth and took it again. Swirling it a final time, he returned it to her mouth, then he pulled away, the full length of her tongue gliding over his like the hottest wet velvet.

"That was good," he whispered.

"Quit trying to change the subject," she said on a sigh. Sucking in a quavering breath, she teased, "I know your type because I read the résumés from the women you were going to interview for Cindi's job."

Rafe winced. This wasn't the first time Mackinley had made him feel...guilty? Caught? Immature? Rafe wasn't sure, but he suddenly wished Shark hadn't gotten everyone to use an agency where the résumés came with eight-by-ten color glossies. "Well," he said, his lips twisting with irony as his fingers stroked Mackinley's waist, "they all typed at least twenty words a minute."

"Maybe they *were* twenty years old."

"Maybe those are just the kind of women a man wants in the office," Rafe countered, feeling the cool, raw seductive silk of her scarf against his rough stubbly cheek as he leaned to nuzzle her neck. "Maybe there are other kinds of women a man needs..." His voice trailed off.

"In bed?" Mackinley finished.

Leaning back, he squinted, hardly believing she was coming on to him like this. "Are you trying to seduce me, sweetheart?"

Her lipstick-blurred lips curved irresistibly upward. "Maybe."

"You're doing a fine job of it," he admitted. "But do you mind if I ask why?" He'd been seriously mean to her ever since she started working at Ransom High Risk.

She shrugged. "Why not? Life's full of surprises."

"You're definitely one of them," he admitted, still feeling stunned at discovering the effect she had on him. He cleared his throat. "So, why don't you tell me what you see in me?"

"Maybe I'm taking you on as a charity case," she said, her mouth tilting playfully.

"Charity case?" Biting back a smile, he stared deeply into her eyes, the soft velvet irises looking glossy and luminous in the low light.

"You know," she volleyed back. "Maybe I'm from Save the Whales. Or the Animal Rescue League."

Rafe winced again, damning himself for overreacting to her suggestions about taking free-of-charge cases. At the slight tensing of her body, Rafe's chest got strangely, unexpectedly tight. He suspected his sheer body size was making her nervous and he wished it didn't. He suddenly wanted to tell her how much he wanted her, that he'd spend the time necessary for her to get used to the feel of him, but it was awkward to say something like that. "Tomorrow at work," he found himself murmuring, "we'll go over those charity cases again. I never mind taking on some extra work."

She bit back a grin. "I said *you're* the charity."

That'll be the day. Still, she was jerking his chain, and Rafe was surprised to find himself loving it. "Me? Let me guess. Am I the whale in Save the Whales?"

Sliding a hand up his shirtfront, she toyed with his tie. "No. Maybe you're an animal from the Animal Rescue League."

"Maybe."

"Anyway, Shark said you just broke up with a woman named Charmaine." Mackinley's sudden soft chuckle held a trace of nervous embarrassment. "So, maybe I've decided to help you get back into action. See? I've been checking up on you."

He should have felt angry. Instead he sucked in a breath as stubby fingers that shouldn't have felt so sexy drummed on his chest. What was the woman trying to do, kill him with lust? At the touch of her bitten-down fingertips, his groin had flexed; his blood rushed and his fingers stilled on her waist. "Shark was talking to you about my love life?"

Mischievous lights were in her eyes. "Such as it is."

Rafe couldn't help but laugh. "Lately my love life would make for a short conversation."

"You don't sound too depressed about it."

"I'm not." Leaning closer, bending his knees and arching his hips, Rafe let his eyes drift over her features. Somehow, he couldn't believe he was standing here, wanting to talk about his last relationship with Mackinley. "Well, Charmaine's long gone. That much I can tell you."

Mackinley's already raspy voice lowered in a way

that would have encouraged the most tight-lipped male, and her eyes tilted up to his, looking brown, bright and curious. "Did you love her?"

The question took him by surprise. He considered a moment. "No." He glanced away, his gaze skating around the darkened chipped floor tiles before returning to her eyes, which seemed even prettier in the lobby's low light than they had under the fluorescent lights at work. "Charmaine was an ex-assistant of Shark's," Rafe explained. "She left to take a job doing billboards for Big Boss Sneakers."

Mackinley's eyes widened. "Shark told me she was a jazz singer."

"That was before Big Boss Sneakers."

Mackinley looked worried. "Charmaine's the practically naked blonde on the billboards? The one completely draped in what looks like cheesecloth?"

"She's also wearing sneakers," Rafe pointed out. "Anyway, she's got a wild family—they live up in the Bronx—and last year, she needed help convincing a loan shark uptown not to kill her little brother."

Mackinley offered a mock-glum frown. "She was beautiful, talented *and* in need of male aid?"

Rafe nodded. "Yes. Her brother is fine—Shark and I payed his debt—but Charmaine and I didn't end well. Which is why I've closed the door on charity cases."

"She hurt you that badly?"

Rafe shook his head. "Not really. I just thought..." He paused, wondering why he felt so compelled to tell Mackinley about Charmaine.

Her voice was interested, coaxing. "Thought?"

"I started thinking about settling down, I guess." Offering a wry smile, he glanced over his shoulder through the lobby door at the busy Manhattan street. "Maybe I'm getting too old for late nights around town. We were only together six months...and then, a few months back, she wound up going back to her old boyfriend."

Mackinley's voice was barely audible. "Why?"

"At first we ran around, mostly hitting new restaurants, and lots of jazz clubs, since she knows industry people."

"Sounds exciting."

"Not really." Something had happened about which even Rafe's own father was unaware; Rafe had begun to want more from a woman. Ever the party girl, Charmaine hadn't exactly been compliant. And as much as Rafe was hesitant to admit it, it was the first time he'd ever been ditched, much less thrown over for another man. Now his voice turned low, throaty. "How long's it been for you, baby?"

Mackinley's breath caught as he dragged his gaze down her face, taking in her eyes, the smattering of barely-there freckles and lips that tasted of menthol. Lifting a hand from her waist, he slipped it under her lapel, so he could rub her shoulder. She said, "Been?"

He leaned so near that he could feel the warmth of her breath on his cheek. "Since your divorce, since you've been with somebody."

"Longer than I wanted it to be."

Then let's not waste anymore time. "Good answer." He exhaled a long, slow breath. "Mackinley, I've got to tell you, I can barely believe what's happening here. In my experience, women like you don't...don't come on like this."

She released a raspy, throaty laugh that he felt in his bones. "I haven't moved a muscle."

"Sweetheart," he said. "You don't have to." Conscious of the dark, quiet foyer, Rafe suddenly imagined pulling her under the stairwell. He could almost feel her slender, trembling thighs hugging him, and the blessed relief he'd feel being inside her. A deep rumble rose in his throat and Rafe's green eyes smouldered, burning into hers. Mackinley was hotter than an oven; everything about her sizzled and burned. "My old man didn't have a clue."

She curled her small hands over Rafe's shoulders. "He thinks you need a woman."

"He's right. I need a woman. I need you."

"After Charmaine, I might be too respectable."

Her teasing tone was making him want her more than he'd ever wanted any woman. Bending and capturing her lips for another full-mouthed kiss, Rafe glided a hand over her ribs, just grazing a breast before stroking and cupping her neck again, the simple touch making them both shudder. His usual tough-guy show was fading fast. "Mackinley," he confessed, feeling amazing she was letting him touch her like this, "I have a big secret."

"What?"

"I *like* respectable."

She laughed. "Not what you said earlier at the office."

"A man can change his mind." Proving it, Rafe brought his lips to hers again, the kiss slow and circular now, the pleasure intense and satisfying. It was the kind of kiss he liked best because it led to the kind of sex he liked best, the slow-building kind that lingered until dawn. Tilting his head back, Rafe rubbed his knuckles tenderly against a cheek that felt cool and dewy. He wished he knew why Mackinley was seducing him. Looking to get her feet wet, he wondered, after her divorce? If so, he was glad she'd picked him. "What do you think about going to my place?" he suggested huskily. "We could order dinner in. Maybe your mom can watch the baby all night, and we'll..."

She looked worried now. "Maybe...maybe tomorrow, Rafe."

Tomorrow! He couldn't wait! Flexing his fingers reflexively on her waist as if she might somehow get away, he softly groaned his protest. "But I want to be with you tonight..."

Her dark eyes looked liquid and steamy. "I'm so glad Rafe," she began, "because..." She blushed. "Well, you see...I need help, Rafe."

Oh, don't we all. Her pleading fingers dug into his shoulders. "I know, baby," he assured her raggedly. Whatever her special needs, he'd be pleased to provide.

Relief flooded her features, and he stared down at where his whiskers had reddened her cheeks and where smeared lipstick formed a fuzzy pink line around her mouth. She said, "You do, Rafe?"

"Sure," he managed, his eyes whisking over her hair, his mind fast-forwarding to how he might thread his fingers in the curling golden strands. "I understand. And I'll help get you fixed up right away."

She frowned. "But how did you know? How did you guess?"

Grinning, Rafe blew out another shaky breath. She was so small, so delicate, like a flower. He smoothed the top of her head with his chin, enjoying the feel of the silken lengths before pressing a kiss to her forehead and experiencing a rush of tenderness such as he'd never felt. His gaze captured hers once more. "I know because it's written all over you, Mackinley. Your eyes...well, at the office they're always drifting where they shouldn't—not that I mind—and right now, you *are* melting against me."

She didn't sound happy about it, despite their kisses. "You think I'm talking about sex."

Disappointment coursed through him. "You're not?"

Mackinley was looking out of sorts now, and neither of them was smiling anymore. "Oh, Rafe," she murmured, uncurling her hands from his shoulders and clasping them against her chest. "I just don't know. This is all moving so fast."

"Don't worry," he reassured her in a tender tone he hadn't even known he possessed, feeling sure he understood. "It's okay to only want sex." Twining his fingers with hers, he brought one of her hands down and held it against his thigh. Feeling her fingers so near his fly, Rafe shuddered and he was rewarded with hearing another of her shaky breaths. Lifting his free hand, he cupped her chin. "My guess is you got hurt real bad by your ex, is that right, Mackinley?"

She nodded. "That's a way of putting it."

But in her marriage, Rafe guessed, she'd discovered she had needs that still wanted satisfaction. "I'm sorry things didn't work out," he said smoothly, "but now you've got to start thinking about yourself, Mackinley." His voice deepened with conviction. "There's no need for you to be alone. You can find a willing partner. You can take what you want from a man."

She licked against her dry lips. "You think so, Rafe?"

"I know," he promised, pressing his lips to hers again. And then he simply moaned. "Just kissing you makes me so hot, Mackinley," he whispered hoarsely, dragging his fingertips over her ribs again and lifting a breast from beneath. They both gasped as he used a thumb to circle a tight nipple, and he loved how her breath became fast and labored. "See," he whispered. "It feels good, doesn't it, Mackinley?"

"Yes," she whispered shakily. "It most certainly does."

Suddenly, he bent and bit at her lower lip with sweet, savage hunger. Soon, he was going to taste every inch of Mackinley Leigh. Soon, he was going to give her everything she'd been missing since the breakup of her marriage. Soon...

"Is that you and Rafe Ransom, dear?"

The voice floated down the stairs with the rapid click-clack of high-heels. Rafe leaned back, feeling a flash of anger at having to relinquish the mound of flesh in his hand. His body felt sluggishly thick with desire, and as he offered one last loving squeeze, Mackinley's knife-sharp intake of breath announced she was in the same state as he. She jerked her head toward the stairs just as Rafe lifted his eyes.

And found himself staring at her mother.

3

WHEN PUSH CAME to shove, Rafe could differentiate a cocktail fork from a corncob skewer, but trying to negotiate the Leighs' fancy, slender-stemmed sterling served as a sore reminder that life on the road hadn't been charm school; ex-mercenary dads didn't exactly stockpile arsenals of p's and q's, and the hours Rafe had squandered over the past few years, bumming around Atlantic City casinos with Jack, Shark and Silencer hadn't further honed his table manners.

But maybe Jack was right. Maybe it was time Rafe got over Charmaine and found a steady girlfriend who could turn him into a more couth individual. Business-wise, Rafe did fine, of course. He had plenty of money, good suits, and he could always talk the talk. In fact, he had a meeting first thing tomorrow with some power people from a chichi Midtown ad agency, no problem.

But women-wise, Rafe was used to wild, easy and free, and until Charmaine, he was used to getting his way. *He* was usually the one who left. Now he realized he hadn't had dinner with a woman's family since he'd first visited the Biancos, after which he'd— perhaps foolishly—saved Charmaine's brother from slow, certain death. Charmaine's gratitude, of course, had been short-lived. Six months later, with her brother still out of the weeds and Rafe pushing her to spend more evenings at home with him, she'd run for higher ground—a penthouse on Eighty-fourth Street owned by her ex, a car dealer named Freddie Ricardo. That Rafe's rival had the same surname as the guy on *I Love Lucy* hadn't helped matters. Nor had the Big Boss Sneaker contract, since Charmaine's head had ballooned the instant she signed on the dotted line. Ballooned, Rafe thought now. Ha. It had become the size of a zeppelin.

But that was all ancient history.

Fighting the urge to rest his elbows on the Leighs' dainty lace tablecloth, Rafe's eyes strayed to Mackinley, and he decided she was as out of his league as Babe Ruth on a softball field. Sure, Rafe probably had the cushier bank account, but Mackinley had all the class. Unlike most women he knew, she wasn't even looking to expose her delectable body to photographers for cold hard cash. But why was she coming onto him? Was she slumming it? Looking for a quick affair on the rebound from her ex? For great sex with no fear of commitment? Rafe should have been thrilled at the idea, but he was...vaguely offended. Okay, he admitted. So, maybe he *was* dark and swarthy, but that didn't mean he was good for one thing only. Right? Besides, it didn't fit. Mackinley seemed like the marrying kind.

"Is your name really Rafael?" Mackinley's mother, Barbara, began in a genteel, cultured voice, interrupting his train of thought. "What a beautiful name."

"My mother chose it." Rafe shrugged. "I was named after her father, but everybody calls me Rafe."

"Ah." Barbara sighed airily as if he'd said something particularly satisfactory, and then her eyes—soft brown eyes that were very like Mackinley's—trailed over a heart-shaped Valentine centerpiece from which two long red tapers flickered. "Look," she continued, "Kimmie's pointing at you again. He wants you to hold him, Rafe. Isn't that the sweetest thing you've ever seen?"

"Definitely one of them," Rafe assured her.

Leaning toward the high chair between her and Mackinley, Barbara playfully pinched her grandson's cheek. "Are you in need of male influence, dear?" Giggling, the baby clapped, then happily swirled a sticky-fingered hand in cold mashed peas and yams.

"Mother," Mackinley warned, her cheeks coloring.

"Well, Kimmie never gets to be around men, do you, Kimmie? Rafe, you're the first man Mackinley's brought home since...since her divorce."

"Rafe won't help with Kimmie," Mackinley replied darkly, appearing embarrassed by her mother's comments. With a quick flirtatious smile, she added, "Not unless you want your grandson to learn the fine art of scar description embellishment, so he can impress girls."

Glancing at Barbara, Rafe decided matchmaking was a genetically hard-wired parental trait. "Knife-throwing 101," he added mildly. He'd shrugged out of his jacket, exposing the short-sleeved shirt he was wearing even though it was February, and when Mackinley stared at the ring of dark leaves circling his left biceps, he flexed the muscle.

She said, "And then you move on to your tattoo seminar?"

Rafe shot her a devilish grin. "Are you kidding? After the knives, we start swallowing flaming swords and breaking boards with our heads." He chuckled softly. "Well," he amended. "Only if our able-bodied assistant has survived."

Mackinley laughed. "Ah. I guess every knife-throwing event requires a scantily clad assistant. But can you really break boards with your head?"

Now she seemed genuinely curious, so he answered truthfully. "Yeah." His shoulders shook with repressed merriment. "But it hurts. I'd rather be juggling cats."

She nodded. "Hmm. And you live on beer and pretzels at home, I imagine?"

"Oh," he promised, "I throw in a few shots of tequila."

Mackinley looked thoroughly amused, her kissable lips pursing in pleasure, her eyes sparkling in the candlelight. "It's always good to have a well-balanced diet." She held up a staying hand. "And don't tell me. It's the worm you like most."

Rafe bit down twice, his strong white teeth flashing. "Like they say, he's three of the four food groups."

"I'm afraid to ask, but what's the fourth?"

Rafe surveyed her solemnly. "Beer nuts."

"Oh, dear me!" Barbara offered a soft, tittering half-scandalized laugh.

"Well," Mackinley said. "Just don't teach my son about brandings and piercings tonight while I'm gone, I'm begging you."

Rafe rolled his eyes, liking the banter, liking that Mackinley was so quick-tongued. Some women simply didn't understand the fine art of verbal foreplay.

"Nice to know you've got such a high opinion of my mentoring skills," he said, doing his best to neatly fold his napkin before he placed it beside his plate. Glancing down, he realized it looked as wrinkled as a shar-pei dog. He just wished Mackinley's presence wasn't dulling his mind, which was usually sharp as a tack. Rifling a hand through his thick, black hair, he squinted at the baby again. "I'm really sorry," he said in apology. "When we got here, I did think Kimmie was a..."

"Girl?" Barbara chuckled.

"Open mouth. Insert foot," chided Mackinley.

Rafe shrugged. "I don't know much about babies, and I confess, they all kind of look alike."

"Looked alike," corrected Mackinley. "Before my son."

"Right," Rafe amended.

"Oh, don't be silly." Barbara reached to pat Rafe's hand, and he was surprised to find he enjoyed the brief, maternal intimacy. "It is hard to tell when they're this age, Rafe," she assured him.

As if he'd know. "Well," he found himself returning with a smile, aware he wanted Mackinley's mother to like him, "you look way too young to be a grandmother."

Mackinley smirked. "Flattery will get you anywhere."

Barbara smiled. "Indeed it will. Thank you, Rafe. I do believe that's the nicest thing anyone's said to me for a while."

"Pleased to hear it." Leaning back in his chair, Rafe relaxed, watching Barbara as she used the back of a hand to push away long, fallen tendrils of frosted upswept hair. She dipped a linen napkin in a pewter water glass and began wiping Kimmie's fingers. Rafe didn't know what to make of her yet. She shared Mackinley's brown eyes and determined jaw, but her expression was somehow resigned, as if she'd given up on life—maybe because she'd lost her husband, Carter, last year.

Rafe took a deep breath. It was obvious to him, from Mackinley's brief references to her father, that she and her dad had been close, and her personal loss weighed heavily on him. As mad as he was at Jack right now, Rafe was damned if he had any idea what he'd do without him.

Mackinley was eyeing him. "You thought Kimmie was a girl, huh?"

"Well, he's..." Wearing fussy lavender pajamas and his favorite toy's a doll. "Uh, his name's Kim?" *Isn't that a girl's name?*

"Kimball George Leigh," Barbara announced proudly. "They're all family names."

Taking a pinch of unfinished meat loaf from a gilt-edged china plate, Mackinley slipped the crumbs between Kimmie's lips, then lifted him from the high chair and cuddled him against her chest. "Now that he's starting to talk," she said, gazing down at the baby, "we're trying to come up with something more..."

"Masculine," said Barbara with a smile. "I've been trying to think..."

Mackinley smiled. "Me, too."

Rafe didn't trust himself to say anything. Mackinley's husky, whispery voice was still lingering in his ears, and he couldn't help but react to how pretty she looked with the baby. Shadows of candle flames were flickering on her cheeks, and she was smiling down lovingly, almost reverently. The soft light played on the licks of her golden hair, seeming to wreathe her head with light as if she was wearing a halo. Fighting the urge to tell her she looked angelic, Rafe wished he could remember his own mother, and he wondered if she'd ever held him the way Mackinley held Kimmie; she must have. Rafe's throat got unexpectedly tight and he glanced away. Hard to believe he'd never known his own mother, that a woman he couldn't even recall had loved him as much as Mackinley Leigh obviously loved her son. Had she given her husband this same devotion? Rafe wondered, glancing at her again. Did she still have such feelings, ready to bestow on another man? Given how hot and willing she'd felt downstairs in his arms, her marriage hadn't soured her on the opposite sex. Her mouth, teasing his, had been way sassier than it looked, and now he ached to feel it elsewhere on his body. Her breast had felt so right, too, so heavy in his hand, her shudders so promising.

And now the woman looked like a goddess.

Seeming to sense the burning intensity of his gaze, Mackinley glanced up. Their eyes met and held, just a moment too long, and his chest constricted. Blowing out a sigh, he shifted his focus, trying to concentrate on the mystery posed by the Leighs' apartment. The place was as hard to read as a crime scene, or the slippery kidnappers Rafe dealt with on the job.

What were two such Waspy-looking women doing in a dump like this? The heavy furniture and expensive lamps were at odds with the torn linoleum and cheap window blinds. And who'd ever heard of serving meat loaf at a table set for kings? Deciding the women had experienced a comedown after Carter Leigh's death, Rafe's mood darkened. Hadn't the man provided for them in his will? Had he left debts? If so, why hadn't Mackinley used her skills and education to find a better-paying job?

Rafe's eyes narrowed watchfully as Barbara smoothed the lace tablecloth with the flat of her hand; the gesture seemed tentative, even nervous. Like her daughter, Barbara had small fingers that fidgeted, although hers had fingernails which hadn't been chewed to the quick. At first Rafe had thought Barbara was anxious about his moving in for a week—any woman in her right mind would be—but Barbara kept saying she was thrilled to have him. He just didn't get it.

And he was intrigued. Rafe wished he wasn't, especially since this first-night dinner scene held shades of Charmaine. None of the guys knew that during the Charmaine saga, Rafe's thoughts had U-turned to settling down and Charmaine had fled—and now Rafe feared he was inviting rejection again. Still, he couldn't keep his gaze from Mackinley.

Or Kimmie. It didn't take a brain surgeon to realize the Leigh women were envisioning a lifetime of debate teams and chess clubs for the boy, not to mention a wardrobe of navy blazers and penny loafers. Fine, Rafe thought, if they could afford private schools down the road. But if the kid was enrolling here on the Lower East Side, he'd be better off with a good set of brass knuckles or numchucks.

"Would you mind holding him, Rafe?" Mackinley asked, drawing him from his thoughts as she rose and circled the table. "No...uh, really I don't think..." Rafe managed.

She nestled the baby's cushioned, diapered behind on Rafe's knee and guided Rafe's hand around the baby's back. Rafe's heart did a three-sixty in his chest. "I don't think I've ever held a baby." And this one was wobbling. Pressing a hand to Kimmie's belly, Rafe tried to hold him in place.

Barbara was astounded. "Not once?"

Not a lot of babies in American overseas schools. Rafe shook his head. "No." Just those French kids from the bus that had been hijacked, but they were toddlers. Even now, Rafe could feel how their tiny fists had clung to his shoulders as he'd rescued them. As he'd carried them toward their parents, he'd felt his heart was breaking. The kids had been too young to know so much fear.

Mackinley's voice was gentle. "Here. Let me show you. You need to relax a little more, Rafe."

"I'm relaxed," he protested. "But why don't you take him again?"

Ignoring him, Mackinley carefully rearranged Kimmie on Rafe's lap. She straightened the chubby little legs that dangled between Rafe's, and closed her hand over Rafe's again, pressing it more firmly against the tiny, otherwise unsupported back. "He's...uh, little," Rafe managed, his throat feeling unaccountably raw as he stared down at Kimmie, who was clutching a doll.

A doll. Rafe's eyebrows furrowed. Maybe tomorrow, he could pick up some little black jeans and a baseball cap. Kimmie could definitely use other toys, too—trucks and cars, plastic soldiers. Guy stuff. The doll had to go. About the size of a Barbie doll, she had long, once-luxurious brown hair that was now matted, probably from being dragged as the baby crawled. She was stark naked, too, not to mention more anatomically correct than Rafe wanted to notice in mixed company. Kimmie's chubby fingers were closed around her slender plastic ankles in a death grip.

"Well," Rafe ventured, taking his eye off the baby just long enough to glance at Mackinley and her mother. "He's got good taste in women, and obviously knows how to hold on to them." Rafe thought once more of Charmaine, who'd left without a backward glance.

Mackinley laughed. "Not a young man to shy away from commitments."

What about you? Rafe wondered. Are you looking for one? What makes you tick, sweetheart?

Barbara smiled. "The doll's name's G.G., short for Glamour Girl. She's his special lady friend."

Bouncing Kimmie, Rafe leaned down and joked, "I'm partial to blondes myself." *Petite, golden-haired blondes.*

"Don't worry, Mom, you'll find another job," Mackinley was saying, returning to a previous subject. Rafe half listened, gingerly shifting Kimmie on his knee, and when the baby cooed, Rafe felt an unexpected rush of pleasure. As it turned out, holding babies wasn't so bad, after all.

"Carter would be so upset," Barbara said, worriedly flexing the fingers of her clasped hands. "But the phone system at work was so complicated, Mackinley. It was a whole switchboard, like something you'd expect to see at a phone company. And the boss got so mad at me in front of everyone at the office. It was humiliating...." Barbara's voice trailed off. "Things have changed so much since I last had a job, and I don't have useful experience anymore."

"You volunteered at Saint Vincent's when Dad was alive," Mackinley reminded. "And in Saint Luke's secondhand clothing shop, remember, Mom?"

Gently rubbing Kimmie's back, Rafe frowned. The hospital and church were in Greenwich Village. Had the Leighs lived there? If so, when did they move to the Lower East Side. And why? Rafe made a mental note to check back issues of phone directories tomorrow for their previous address.

"But that's the second job I've lost, and now I've got to go back to the headhunter first thing tomorrow." With a fleeting, embarrassed glance at Rafe, Barbara continued, "Are you sure you don't mind dropping Kimmie at day care in the morning?"

"My pleasure." Rafe had offered during dinner.

"You're such a nice man," Barbara murmured. "I'm just glad Carter's not alive to see all this."

All what? wondered Rafe. What exactly had happened here?

Mackinley's cheeks flushed as she shot Rafe an apologetic glance. Obviously, she didn't like including outsiders in family business, but Rafe wished he knew more. "Daddy would have been proud of you, Mom."

"Ouch. Don't hurt me," Rafe suddenly said, frowning down. Giggling, Kimmie gleefully beat G.G. against Rafe's shoulder, her brown hanks of mottled hair flying. Snuggling the baby closer, Rafe looked around. Pictures of Carter Leigh were everywhere, mostly family vacation snapshots depicting better times. Why weren't the women more forthcoming about what had happened to them? Why had they ignored Rafe's gentle probes during dinner?

Something strange was going on. When Rafe testified against kidnappers in court, he always got this same feeling. Lawyers and judges dickered behind the scenes about what was admissible, so the truth wound up feeling as slippery as a buttered eel. Here, Rafe was sure the Leigh women had been whispering in the kitchen about what he should—or shouldn't—be told.

Peering down at Kimmie, Rafe thoughtfully chewed the inside of his cheek. The baby stared back, his eyes as innocent and trusting as his mother's. Suddenly, his lips puckered and Rafe tensed, ready to hand him over to someone who could deal with tears. But then the baby smiled.

Just for me, Rafe thought.

He hunched his shoulders, ducked and smiled back.

Kimmie made a sound resembling giggling.

Rafe's smile broadened. "I see we have an understanding."

Barbara turned to Rafe. "Would you mind having him in your room? The crib's next to Mackinley's bed, and it would be easier not to move it."

Rafe tensed, and the baby frowned with concern. "Doesn't he need...diapers and bottles or something?"

"He's a great baby," Barbara assured him. "He'll sleep right through the night, just the way Mackinley did." Barbara paused, smiling indulgently at her daughter in a way that made Rafe think again of his own mother. "Unless you mind, Rafe?"

It was the least Rafe could do, given how his father had foisted him onto Barbara, but Barbara's easy acceptance of this situation made Rafe's mind start whirring again. Were Mackinley and Barbara serious about going through with this? "I'm flexible," he said with a quick glance at Mackinley. "I'm used to staying with strangers while I'm working."

Mackinley's smile suddenly turned doubtful. "With babies?"

"Well no." He added, "However, last year I did spend a full four months with a family in Mexico City." Rafe decided not to mention that the head of the household had been kidnaped by a drug lord, and although Rafe had managed to negotiate a release, the man had nearly died from weight loss, dehydration and the effects of psychological torture suffered during captivity.

Life suddenly sparkled in Barbara's eyes. "Once Carter went to Mexico City on business," she said.

"Rafe travels all the time," Mackinley put in.

Barbara smiled. "How lovely. That means you'll fit right in and be comfortable here. I'll do everything I can to make your stay pleasant." Her smile deepened. "I imagine you've got some wonderful slides from your travels, Rafe."

Rafe didn't even own a camera, and it wasn't as if he spent his time touring museums. "Some."

"I spoke Spanish," Barbara enthused. "Oh, it was a long time ago, but I had an interest in languages before I married Carter, which may be why Mackinley studied them in college." Barbara beamed proudly at her daughter. "Her Spanish is wonderful."

"I noticed." She was every bit as fluent as Rafe. Twice since his arrival, angry Spanish-speaking tenants had banged on the Leighs' door, complaining about building maintenance difficulties—as if the Leighs' were responsible for calling the landlord. No doubt, the foreign speakers realized Mackinley was a soft touch, and now they were making liberal use of her as a translator. Rafe's jaw set grimly at the thought.

Mackinley sighed, and there was distress in her eyes as they settled on her son. "Well, I...I guess I'd better be going."

"You should, dear," Barbara said, a catch in her voice. Obviously, she didn't want her daughter to leave, so why wasn't she stopping her?

Mackinley rose with a sigh, and Rafe inhaled deeply as he watched her move. She was petite, but full-figured, with hips and breasts that swayed like a woman's should. She'd pushed up the sleeves of the chocolate sweater, and seeing the unblemished skin of her lower arms, Rafe wanting nothing more than to rub his thumb along the silky undersides. Then, his tongue. No way, he suddenly thought, was Mackinley Leigh leaving him with her mother and baby tonight. "I'll walk you to the door."

"Please, don't get up, Rafe. I still have to finish getting my things together."

Mackinley swiftly circled the table, briefly kissed Kimmie then beelined for the door, but not before Rafe saw the sudden flash of pain in her eyes. He frowned. She definitely didn't want to leave her son.

"I'd better clear the table," Barbara announced, standing and whisking away Rafe's plate. As she pushed through a swinging door to the kitchen, her voice caught once more as she called, "Be sure to pack a warm nightgown, dear."

From the hallway, Mackinley called, "Already did, Mom."

"What's going on here, kid?" Rafe whispered to Kimmie. When Kimmie chortled, he continued, "So, you're not talking, either, huh?" During dinner, Barbara had asked about the Ransom's agency, so, she knew enough to assume Rafe was a professional good guy, but Rafe still couldn't believe she was willing to be left alone with a stranger.

Carefully resettling Kimmie on his hip and wrapping a massive arm comfortably around the baby's back, Rafe went in search of Mackinley. She was standing in front of the scarred metal apartment door, her coat on, tugging a cute dark knit hat down to her sparse honey-colored eyebrows.

"Getting ready to rob something?" he asked.

She looked startled, almost guilty. "What?"

"The hat. It looks like bank-robbing attire."

She forced a laugh. "Oh."

He might have further considered her guilty expression, but seeing the two carryon bags on the floor somehow rankled; she hadn't even seriously considered Rafe's proposition that they stay at his apartment together. "Is it because of your mom?"

She frowned. "My Mom?"

He lowered his voice to a husky whisper. "That you don't want to spend the night with me?"

In the dim light and against her pale skin, Mackinley's eyes looked even darker, the almost-black color of dusty charcoal, and they held a mix of trust and expectancy that Rafe didn't quite understand. "Since Mom and I started living together," she admitted, "I've never stayed out all night. So...we'd better do what we're supposed to tonight, Rafe."

Smiling as the baby's wet, clammy fingers started exploring his inner ear cavity, Rafe peered harder into Mackinley's eyes, hoping his gaze communicated pure heat. "Downstairs," he found himself coaxing silkily, "it seemed clear what we're supposed to do tonight. Not that staying with your mom won't be fine."

He was glad that made Mackinley smile. "She's nice, huh?"

"Seems that way." His voice dropped another notch. "But you're nicer, sweetheart. Much nicer." He slid his free hand inside her coat and under the hem of her sweater, loving the way she tensed as he stroked the bare skin of her waist. "I wanted to be with you, Mackinley. Tonight." His eyes dragged down her face, resting where her lips parted in nervous anticipation. "But then," he added, "some things are worth the wait. And I know we hardly know each other. Yet."

Dishes clanked, and they both glanced toward the kitchen.

He said, "Your mom's clearing the table."

Mackinley's voice caught. "Maybe I should go help her."

"No, sweetheart," Rafe whispered. "Stay and help me."

Holding Kimmie tightly, Rafe smoothed a palm over Mackinley's hip, then over her backside until his fingers curled under a cheek—all the way down, into the sweet crevice where it met her thigh. Finding warmth there, he sucked in a sharp breath of agony, then locked his mouth on hers, drawing her tongue deeply between his lips. When he withdrew, he whispered, "I wanted that kiss all during dinner."

"So did I. Maybe tomorrow night..."

"I'll be looking forward to it." A final time, his mouth claimed hers, his probing tongue now exploring her more fully. Eliciting a shiver, he shut his eyes and deepened the kiss, his tongue lapping, his consciousness dragging downward to oblivion. Kissing Mackinley Leigh had turned out to be heaven. And just as surely, it was hell. Already, Rafe had heard too many protests. He wanted silence. Darkness. And then whimpers and moans. He wanted to do things to her that no man had ever done, not even her husband. Judging from the shakiness of her voice, he already was.

"Please," she murmured, her hands resting on his chest. "I've got to go, Rafe."

He was surprised to hear the roughness, the need, in his own voice. "If you don't go soon, I might not let you, you know." He chuckled softly. "I'll clutch you by the ankles, the way Kimmie does with G.G."

Taking him at his word, she whispered, "I know," and quickly slipped from where he'd pinned her against the door, a raspy catch sounding in her throat when her eyes settled on Kimmie. "I've never left him for the night," she suddenly confessed, pain deepening the color of her eyes. "Not even once. He's on a bottle, so it's okay, but..."

"Damn," Rafe cursed softly, feeling a flash of temper. She was such a sincere woman and an honest employee. And now, all because of his dad's harebrained attempts at matchmaking, she was going to be separated from her baby for the first time. He readjusted Kimmie, lifted a hand and lightly brushed a thumb against her cheek. "C'mon, sweetheart. You don't have to leave him. In fact, I don't want you to. We don't have to trade places. We both know my dad hasn't been acting right since that synergy workshop."

That got a smile out of her. "Actually," she said, "I think he went a little nuts. But then, I didn't know him before."

"Trust me," said Rafe. "He was mean as a snake. And we all liked him better that way. But what say we just *tell him* we switched?"

Mackinley looked totally shocked. "Lie?"

"Sure," Rafe said easily. "I'll head home, and you can stay right here with your *bambino*."

The eyes she fixed on her son said she wanted nothing more in the world, but it was clear she wasn't going to take Rafe's suggestion. "But we said we'd trade. It's...our *job*."

Rafe shook his head. "Look, Mackinley, you're the most honest woman I've ever met, but you shouldn't have to leave your baby because of my father."

"I'm not that honest," she murmured cryptically.

"Well..." Knowing it was pointless to argue and feeling strangely helpless, Rafe gave up and simply kissed her once more.

"You're nibbling," Mackinley said of the kiss.

"Gearing up for a larger meal," Rafe promised. He glanced down at the baby in his arms. "Don't worry,

I'll take good care of him," Rafe said, and then he realized Mackinley was staring at him with dazed, lust-filled eyes.

"I know," she whispered. "You're really nice, Rafe."

Barbara's voice floated down the hallway. "You still here?"

"On my way out, Mom," Mackinley called. "And thanks for dinner. You know to call me at Rafe's if you need anything."

Her eyes met Rafe's. "I've got to go."

"Wish you weren't."

"Me, too."

He bent, so she could kiss Kimmie goodbye. "You've got my address and keys," Rafe said, still tasting her lips. "Make yourself at home. And... Happy Valentine's Day."

Hugging Kimmie fervently, Mackinley whispered, "Thanks."

And then, as fleeting as their last kiss, she was gone.

Rafe stared after her, shocked over the sudden change in his love life. Half expecting her to return, his eyes remained fixed on the empty exterior hallway and staircase, but she never came back. He closed and locked the apartment door, then glanced down at Kimmie. Big brown curious eyes stared up. "Baba?"

Rafe had no idea what that meant. Mama? Baby? Bye-bye? He shrugged. "That's right," he said, his eyes trailing to where Kimmie still held G.G. in a death grip, now by a mottled hank of hair. "Bye-bye. But don't you worry, Mommy'll be back."

And next time Rafe wasn't going to let her get away.

"THINK," MACKINLEY commanded herself.

But Rafe's kisses were still clouding her mind. So was the fact that he'd been so sweet tonight—polite to her mother, enamored of her son. He didn't know it, but she'd teared up when he wished her a Happy Valentine's Day. His concern over her being away from Kimmie touched her more than anything had in a long time, and when she thought of that, guilt assaulted her. She pushed it aside since she couldn't afford the emotion. She was using Rafe, plain and simple. So, dammit, why did he have to turn out to be so nice?

"C'mon." She stared harder at the blinking dialogue box on Rafe's computer screen, wracking her brain for a password Rafe might have chosen, then she gave up and glanced around. The only Rafe-like thing in Rafe's apartment had turned out to be his refrigerator. Virtually empty, it contained the sort of items Mackinley had imagined: curled pizza crusts, half-empty takeout containers from a nearby Japanese restaurant and imported beer. Nothing edible from any known food group. No tequila, either. And Mackinley definitely could have used a bolstering shot.

She'd found some women's clothes in a closet—most of the items too tight, too short and too colorful. That, she supposed, was to be expected also, and she didn't even want to contemplate the stabs of jealousy she'd felt.

Otherwise, the place was a surprise. She'd anticipated finding dirty gym clothes, heaps of unfolded laundry, and yesterday's trash. But the building was unobtrusively posh, with a uniformed doorman who said Mr. Ransom had kindly phoned to say she was expected. The black marble flooring in the outer hallways gleamed, and vases of fresh flowers were perched on black lacquered tables.

The interior carpeting was muted gray, the living room furniture of black and beige leather. The bedroom was empty, except for the desk where she was seated, an armchair, a bedside table and a king-size bed. Staring past the computer terminal, through a sliding glass door that led to a balcony overlooking Central Park, Mackinley felt a rush of sadness remembering the brownstone where she'd grown up and which had been sold.

No use crying over spilled milk. Reflected in the sliding glass doors, she could see her single carry-on. Rafe's kiss had flustered her so much that she'd walked off without her clothes, taking only the satchel with the money. Tomorrow, she'd have to rush home and change before work.

She stared at the screen again. Apparently, the system required Rafe to update the password each week. "So, what's been on his mind?" She'd already tried numbers she'd found while snooping in his office— his driver's license, social security, address, phone, and bank card numbers.

Now she tried friends and family again. "Shark. Silencer. Magnum. Jack." Giving up, she moved on to whatever Rafe-related terms popped into her head: "Sexy. Big. Nicer than I thought."

"Nothing." She desperately needed this printout. If she asked Rafe to help her and he refused, she'd at least have some new information on kidnappers in South America, which was where she thought Kimmie's dad was. Fingers still poised above the keyboard, she stared outside waiting for inspiration.

"Great," she suddenly sighed, raising her own flagging spirits with plucky irony. "As if there's a kidnapping muse. I should be so lucky." Beyond the sliding glass doors, the velvet winter night sparkled with stars, and her eyes trailed around the low stone wall circling the park. Weak yellow light from tall, black, wrought-iron lamps partially illuminated ominous stone steps leading downward. Suddenly nervous, she shifted her gaze to the cell phone next to the mouse pad. The phone hadn't rung since she'd been in the Humvee. But it would. Usually the calls came in twos or threes. By the third call, the kidnappers would give her instructions.

She hoped it wasn't tonight. It was too cold, too dark, and the drop sites were always scary. She'd brought the forty thousand dollars, though. Carrying it here had unnerved her—she kept imagining a purse snatcher taking the bag, but if a call came in the middle of the night, she couldn't return to her apartment for the money, not with Rafe there.

"I can't take much more of this."

Months ago, after forking over almost all her family's assets, she'd been sure the kidnappers would return Oliver. Instead, they'd begun nickel-and-diming her, seemingly knowing exactly how much money she had left. Had they accessed information about her financial status through computers? She knew hackers could do almost anything nowadays. Or had they coerced Oliver into talking about her bank balances?

What if they'd tortured him? A sudden whimper escaped her. Oliver had been an investment banker and had often conducted business in countries experiencing political trouble. After he'd disappeared during a trip to South America, she'd received pictures of him holding various Spanish-language newspapers, all of which she'd identified by research. None of the particular papers were regularly sold in the U.S. which narrowed the field.

Eyeing the phone, she fought the urge to call her mom, to make sure Kimmie was okay, but calling would only distract her from breaking into Rafe's database. "I wouldn't mind hearing Rafe's voice, either," she whispered. Until tonight, she'd never really noticed how low and deep it was, both chesty and smooth, like comforting background music that you recognized, but didn't necessarily know the words to.

"Danger," Mackinley whispered as she typed. "Rafe."

And then her mind drew another blank. Feeling her heart palpitate with panic, she blinked back tears as she thought about the incredible amounts of money she'd electronically transferred to overseas accounts earlier in the year, a fortune her father had worked his entire life to build. Not that she—or her mom—cared about money. They just wanted Oliver back. She might be divorced, but the ink had barely been dry on the divorce papers when Oliver had been kidnapped, and he'd never even seen his son. *Besides, you want more explanations about what went wrong...don't you Mackinley?*

"What is the password?" she whispered, pushing aside thoughts of her failed marriage. What if she'd done the wrong thing all along? Acted like a fool? What if Oliver was already dead? Would she ever know if there was anything she could have done to save her marriage?

Once more, she thought of Rafe. Watching him with the baby, she'd seen a gentler, hidden side of him. And when he kissed her at the door, she felt as if she'd been temporarily awakened from her nightmare. The gentle crush of his mouth had made her wonder if— when all this was over—she could accept the failure of her marriage and move on with another man. Rafe was an unlikely partner, but her eyes strayed to the bed where a black quilted cover was turned back on black silk sheets, and she wished he was here, holding her. What would it feel like to make love with a man like him...to hold him naked, the smooth, rock-hard muscles of his back rippling beneath her fingers? So many times tonight she'd almost told him everything. She would have, but she needed to break into his computer first.

But how?

Thrusting a thumb to her mouth, she chewed on the already ragged nail. What had been on Rafe's mind over the past week or so? On impulse, she typed in her own name, then sucked in a quick breath, her eyes widening. "Damn if the man didn't use my name."

The dialogue box blinked, the screen went black, and a computerized voice now said, "Welcome to Wide World Access." A world map appeared, pin-point dots surfaced on it, then broken lines arched between the dots, tracing from country to country. Mackinley read a drop-down list of options, then found a search prompt, where one could find kidnappers by location.

Following the prompts, she began exploring links and cross-references. "Rafe," she said, admiring the database. "You're brilliant." And he had an eye for detail. At first glance, he seemed nothing more than a big lug of a guy, but despite how she'd teased him, Mackinley knew he was mostly responsible for creating Ransom High Risk. The business concept was so new and the clientele so private that it had taken her months of research to even find out such an agency existed. Excitedly, she pulled up lists of names, quickly reading rap sheets and biographical information. She was so immersed that the ringing phone startled her.

She gasped, grabbing it. "Hello? I'm here."

Static sounded, then a rough garbled voice she guessed was coming through a scrambler. She couldn't even tell if it was a man or a woman, much less decide if she was imagining the trace of Spanish accent. "Do you have the fifty thousand?"

Her heart pounded. "You said forty. I've got forty."

"Get another ten tomorrow."

Rage bubbled within her. "I don't have it. And I want to talk to my husband. You haven't let me talk to Oliver for months."

"I know you have more money. Get it or we kill him."

Kill him. Terror seized her as the words echoed in her mind. Maybe she could sell artwork, or the remaining silver. *Oh, Rafe, I wish you were here.* "Where's my husband?"

"Do you want to see him alive or not?"

"Yes. Of course I do." *You've probably killed him already. You keep lying. Are you ever going to quit lying to me?* She'd read everything she could about kidnapping. She knew you weren't supposed to show fear. And if kidnappers realized you'd sought outside help, they often did kill the victim. They had nothing to lose. It was one reason she'd been terrified to approach Ransom High Risk.

The person was talking fast now, maybe trying to get off the phone. "Put the cash in a white plastic bag. Go to Central Park, down the steps to the zoo at Fifth and Sixty-third. At the bottom, place the bag in the green trash barrel on your left, the one with the yellow happy face painted on the side. Turn around, walk away. And don't look back."

The phone went dead.

How did they know she was near Central Park? she thought, panicking. Or did they? Her eyes darted around fearfully. No, her staying near the park was probably unconnected. Rafe's apartment was in the East Seventies, blocks from the zoo.

Thinking that, Mackinley pressed a hand against her chest, right over where her heart was aching and beating out of control. For a brief second, she indulged her wish that this would all be over soon—the panic, the loneliness, the void in her life where love and security had once been—and then she simply ran for Rafe's kitchen, praying she could find a white plastic bag.

"No DOUBT, YOUR Mommy's watching my big color TV," Rafe grumbled, directing the comment toward the crib in the corner, where Kimmie was uttering pathetic, shuddering sob-sighs that Rafe knew were calculated to make him feel guilty.

It was working, too.

Rafe raked his fingers through his hair, then clasped his hands behind his neck. Stretching his legs, he tried to get comfortable, but his cold bare feet poked out the end of Mackinley's short, narrow bed. Grunting, he rolled toward the crib, but the tartan plaid duvet fell away and his exposed elbow slammed against the wall.

His mood darkening, he listened to the groaning plumbing in the walls and pictured Mackinley, seeing her comfortably curled on his black leather sofa, cuddled in his favorite black fuzzy blanket, channel surfing with his remote. "And don't think you can start crying," Rafe suddenly warned.

But it was useless. Soft, lonely-sounding, shaking breaths floated through the dark, hooking on Rafe's heart. He'd offered to move the crib into Barbara's room, or to change rooms with Barbara, but she'd insisted that Kimmie was no trouble. He slept peacefully through the night.

Right.

That must have been before the kid realized he'd found a new sucker to manipulate. "Nine months old," Rafe muttered. "Which means not born yesterday."

A frightened whimper sounded in the dark.

"I'm not that easily coerced," Rafe whispered grumpily.

And then he trained his mind on Mackinley's mother. Barbara was definitely hard to figure. All night, she'd fussed over Rafe as if he was a long lost son; she'd insisted on changing his sheets, then she'd sat quietly while he watched televised sports. She'd offered him so many entertainments—everything from a Scrabble game to dessert—that Rafe had almost broken down and admitted that the only entertainment he felt really desperate for was her daughter.

Kimmie sighed again.

"That's right, kid," Rafe said, thinking Kimmie knew more about hostage negotiation than he did. "Wear down your opponent bit by bit. Go the distance. Appeal to whatever's human in him. Threaten tears and beat him with the doll baby if you have to." Rafe shook his head. "Nine months old. And you're already better at this than half the guys in the office."

Kimmie sniffled loudly.

Rafe snarled, "The last person I met with your staying power was a warlord in South Africa."

Another gasp sounded.

Throwing back the covers, Rafe got up in his underwear, crossed to the crib and lifted out the baby. As he did so, he tried not to notice the sudden swell of his heart. "Damn if you aren't awful small," Rafe said, sounding far angrier than he really felt. "You know that?"

Not fooled by Rafe's seemingly foul disposition, Kimmie cooed pleasantly.

"Aren't you the little manipulator?" Rafe edged around a dresser in the cramped room. He'd gone through the drawers earlier, not feeling the least bit guilty. The raciest things Mackinley owned were waist-high white Hanes cotton briefs, although there were a couple of lace teddies, maybe gifts from her ex—before he was her ex. They looked real sweet and innocent, not to mention barely worn, and Rafe was still trying to decide if that was good or bad.

Because she'd forgotten one of her carry-ons, Rafe had expected her to call, and he'd hated how his heart missed a beat every time the phone rang. But the only two calls were from complaining neighbors; Rafe had wound up flipping a breaker switch for a lady on the fifth floor, then jerry-rigging the hardware of a running toilet up on four.

At least he'd gotten the answer to one of his questions. The Leighs had owned this building and had sold it some months ago, which was ostensibly why the tenants held them responsible for damages. Really, Rafe suspected, they did so because Mackinley was too kindhearted and it was easy to play on her human decency. But why would the Leighs sell? This place was a cash cow, so they must have needed a quick monetary infusion. Had they run into trouble with estate taxes after Carter's death? Whatever the case, Rafe meant to find out.

Kimmie gave a sudden, wheedling gasp as Rafe laid him in bed, sandwiching him between his body and the wall, so he wouldn't fall out. "Oh, right," Rafe muttered, cuddling the kid against his bare chest as he reached for the doll. "Here's G.G."

Kimmie giggled.

Getting a flash of inspiration, Rafe added, "Why don't we call you K.G.? They said they wanted something more macho. It's sort of like K.G.B.," he explained. "Or cagey. Shark would approve."

K.G. nodded acquiescence, clutched his doll, and promptly closed his eyes.

Snuggling his cheek on a pillow, Rafe gently rubbed the baby's lavender-clad tummy, thinking of Mackinley. Two prim flannel nightgowns were in the carryon she'd left, so Rafe figured she must be naked, sliding around on his black silk sheets. The idea brought a slow smile to his lips.

He wished he was there with her, instead of

cramped in her too-small bed. "It's the way she smells," Rafe suddenly whispered, tugging the tartan spread over his muscular shoulder in a way that only served to uncover his backside and legs. Reaching behind himself, he jerked at the covers. "Yeah, maybe it's the way she smells that's driving me so crazy." It was a scent that was hard to describe. Faintly almondy. Clean but musky.

Damn if it wasn't everywhere.

4

LAST NIGHT, Mackinley had forgotten one of her bags, so Rafe thought she might swing by her apartment to change clothes this morning; instead she surprised him by wearing a short, vampy red knit number with a deep V neckline which she'd found in his closet and that belonged to Shark's ex-girlfriend. It didn't look half bad with yesterday's pumps, but better yet, it clung to Mackinley like a second skin, and the amount of leg exposed by a side slit was making Rafe's palms itch. As she leaned in the doorway to his office, the hem hiked another tantalizing inch.

"You're late for work, Ransom."

"If I'd known what you were wearing," he returned, "I would have gotten here a whole lot sooner."

She glanced around, taking in the interior carpet-walled cubicles surrounding the negotiators' windowed offices, then she locked gazes with him again. "I take it you slept in?"

"Or else I'm still in bed," Rafe shot back. "Because as good as you look, sweetheart, I must still be dreaming."

She faked a frown. "Anybody ever tell you that you've got a very quick tongue, Rafe?"

"Other than ex-girlfriends?" Shooting her a grin, he

glanced over his shoulder. Seeing that everybody was still crowded around the empty desk where he'd left K.G., Rafe shoved his hands in the pockets of his best gray suit and ambled toward Mackinley, who fortunately hadn't yet noticed he'd brought her son to work. "I see you've been going through my drawers."

"I...uh, forgot the bag with my skirts, so I hope you don't mind me borrowing the dress?"

"How could I? You're the boss. We've switched places, remember?"

She gazed up at him, smiling. "So, you must be Mackinley."

He smiled back. "And you must be Rafe."

She raised an eyebrow. "But was that a note of fear I detected earlier?"

"Fear?"

She nodded. "Uh-huh. Of reprisal, for how you always make your assistants hop, skip and jump?"

"Absolutely." He laughed and she leaned her head farther back, surveying him, the red dress bringing out the golden-red flecks in her brown eyes, making the smattering of freckles across her nose more pronounced. Rays of white, wintery sunlight streamed over her shoulders from the windows behind her, and he felt a wave of guilt about going through her drawers last night. Compelled to confess, he said, "Anyway, you might want to explain what I found in your apartment."

Her expression darkened, and although the look was fleeting, it lingered long enough to give Rafe pause. She looked half-afraid to ask. "What?"

What don't you want me to find, sweetheart? Suspicion

curled inside him, and once more he tried to tell himself it was nothing more than an occupational hazzard. "White cotton panties," he said in a stage whisper.

Glancing away and rolling her eyes, she seemed relieved, and when she laughed, the sound was so female, so sexy, that Rafe's heart did a flip-flop. Color rose on her cheeks, the color of the pink threads in smooth white marble. "My underthings did a number on you, huh?"

"They did," he admitted even though white panties usually excited him about as much as melba toast. "The clothes belong to Shark's ex-girlfriend," he added. He didn't particularly want to contemplate why he wanted to share that privileged information with Mackinley.

She smirked. "Don't try to weasel out of it. You're busted. Caught in the act. You're entertaining a harem. This dress is definitely too little for Charmaine."

"She's smaller in real life than she looks on the Big Boss billboard," Rafe offered. "But honestly, I was out of the country on a job and Shark was between places, so I let him use my apartment for four months last year."

Mackinley nodded wisely. "And Shark *happened* to break up with his girlfriend while he was there, so then she just *happened* to leave her clothes..."

"It's the truth." Rafe realized he'd spoken too forcefully, but Mackinley's distrusting attitude was getting under his skin, every bit as much as her unwillingness to stay home with the baby last night. "The clothes are Shark's girlfriend's," he repeated. "Really."

"And you," she said, "are known to have a way with words."

"I'm a hostage negotiator. Comes with the territory."

"So, how could I believe a man who's turned a gift for gab into a lucrative career?"

"Really," he said again. "I'm not lying about those being Shark's girlfriend's clothes."

Mackinley's gaze softened and her lips curled in a barely suppressed smile that, somehow, made Rafe want to kiss her good morning. "I know, Rafe. I believe you."

Her obvious amusement tested his ego, but he was relieved anyway. Yes, there was definitely something significant going on between him and Mackinley, and now he knew it was going to involve his emotions. Rafe didn't know how he felt about that yet. Suddenly, his gaze narrowed. "You never thought they were my girlfriends' clothes, did you? You were just jerking my chain, weren't you?"

Mackinley's lips lifted another impish notch, and she held up a thumb and forefinger, her narrowed brown eyes peering at him through the inch of space between. "Maybe a little."

He'd been had. "Hmm."

"Your doorman said Shark stayed in your apartment last year," Mackinley admitted. "And judging from the modeling agency photos and Charmaine, you do go for taller women."

That again. "Only in the past," he declared.

"So," she said, "what's happened since then?" When she cocked her head curiously, a golden lick of hair fell onto her forehead, and when Rafe casually reached over to brush it back into place, the silken touch of it registered so much undeniable heat in his bloodstream that it could have been June, not February.

"Who knows?" His gaze drifted from her hair, down the delicate plane of her cheek and lingered on her mouth. "But lately average height is growing on me as a female feature."

She giggled. It was a nice sound, spontaneous and low, musical and throaty. "You really do have a way with words."

"It's not all I have a way with," Rafe promised.

During the long moment they surveyed each other, Rafe realized it was hopeless. With nothing more than their first kiss, she'd completely turned his head. Why, he didn't know. He'd never felt himself falling so hard, so fast. But he still had a lot of questions about her lifestyle. Especially now that he was fully registering how tired she looked. "Didn't you sleep okay at my place?"

"Fine."

But she hadn't. And seeing the faint dark half moons ringing the puffy space under her eyes, Rafe could have kicked himself. He'd been so taken in by the dress he hadn't even noticed. In fact, now that he thought about it, she often looked tired. It wasn't K.G.'s fault, either; true to Barbara's word, K.G. had slept like a kitten. Rafe's pulse quickened with concern. "Mackinley," he began instinctively. "Is something wrong?"

"Wrong?"

"At home?"

She merely smiled. "How would I know? You're

the one staying there. How were things with my mom?"

Mackinley was sidestepping, and Rafe continued carefully studying her. When it came to liars, he was a pro. Who did the woman think she was dealing with? "Oh, you know, I amused her with my endless repertoire of dirty jokes."

Mackinley slapped his arm playfully. "You did not."

"No," he confessed. "I didn't. But we were like peas in a pod. I really like your mom. Still, sweetheart, I wish you'd stayed home with the baby. I know you missed him." At the words, she glanced away, as if not wanting him to see the painful truth of it in her eyes. So, why hadn't she agreed to lie about trading places so she could stay home? Driven by professional curiosity or attraction—Rafe didn't know which—he felt a renewed compulsion to get to the bottom of the matter.

And then he realized her gaze had landed where the negotiators and assistants were gathered around a desk humoring K.G. "Oh, no, Rafe," she whispered. "You didn't bring him to work."

Rafe squinted at the baby, then shifted his penetrating green eyes to Mackinley. "You're right, Mackinley. I did not."

"Rafe," she warned.

He managed a shrug. "He said he wanted see his fans, his public." Rafe pointed reasonably toward the commotion. "See, look at the crowds. You should be proud. Your son really packs 'em in."

After a moment, Mackinley got that age-old, bemused look that women always get when they watch grown men cook badly or ruin their laundry. Torn between worry and amusement, she didn't want to encourage him, and yet she couldn't help but smile.

"I took him to day care," Rafe explained quickly, seeing her weaken. "But every time I tried to leave, he started crying." Not to mention screaming and clutching Rafe's lapel. Even now, he could see K.G.'s wounded, accusing, frightened brown eyes filling with tears, communicating betrayal, and how his lips had quivered. Besides, Rafe knew Mackinley would be glad to see him. "K.G. really wanted to come," he coaxed.

Mackinley didn't look convinced. "K.G.?"

Rafe nodded. "You and your mom were looking for something more macho than Kimmie."

Mackinley squinted through a gap between Jack, Silencer and Magnum who were beaming and cooing. "What's he wearing?"

Rafe chuckled. He'd stopped at a Chinatown kiosk and bought red plastic sunglasses and a porkpie hat. "The Power Rangers vest is a little much for a Midtown office," Rafe conceded. "But K.G. and I discussed it. After today, he promises only to wear it on casual Fridays. And never to church. Anyway, he seemed to like it. I guess it was still on sale, leftover from Halloween."

Mackinley merely stared at Rafe, as if trying to decide whether or not he was mad.

"Really," Rafe added encouragingly. "Your son pointed at the vest. The only reason he didn't ask me to buy it was because he can't talk."

"My life," whispered McKinley.

"Sometimes women do say I'm impossible," Rafe

commiserated with a smile. "But don't worry. I didn't forget G.G." Proudly, Rafe held up the naked doll, and was glad to see a resigned smile tugging at Mackinley's lips.

"K.G. and G.G., huh?" she said. "Well, I'm glad to see you and my son hit it off."

"We did." Far more than Rafe was ready to admit. Being with the baby had been jarring. This morning, Rafe had awakened to find soulful big brown eyes curiously watching him, and for long moments, he'd gazed back sleepily as K.G. snuggled his tiny hands into Rafe's bushy chest hairs. Then K.G.'s lips had twitched into a friendly, knowing smile. It was like magic. Rafe had never expected to feel it, never imagined it, but suddenly, seeing those small chubby fingers flexing on his chest, Rafe had felt aware of his size, his age, and he'd realized that if he wanted kids, now was the time. Mackinley was watching him curiously, so Rafe said, "For a kid, I guess he's okay."

Her smile was as knowing as her son's. "K.G., huh?" she said again.

Rafe nodded.

"Okay, we'll call him that and see how he likes it. Since he's been learning to talk, Mom and I have been trying to stop calling him Kimmie."

"That's what you said," Rafe returned, his eyes settling on Mackinley's lips. He was about to ask if she'd like to step inside his office for a private kiss good morning when something peripheral caught his eye. Turning, he stared into a windowed conference room, and realized the paper-covered table was laid with coffee and water decanters. A thirtyish woman in a gray suit, her black hair drawn into a complicated braided knot, was delicately nibbling a powdered doughnut and fishing through a glass bowl of wrapped mints. Another woman of about fifty, who was wearing a red suit, appeared in the doorway, anxiously fingering frosted blond bangs. She tapped her watch apologetically. "Sorry, but Leslie and I have another appointment soon," she said. "Is that him? Can we get started?"

"The ad agency meeting," Rafe muttered under his breath. "How could I forget?"

Mackinley raised her voice. "Sorry, Ann," she said, heading for the conference room. "He had trouble with his day care. You know how these single fathers are. I hope you two won't mind having a baby at the meeting." Glancing over her shoulder, she called, "Since my assistant's here, no one else needs to worry about taking notes. Rafe? Why don't you run and get your little notebook?"

MACKINLEY'S EYES widened as a sock-clad toe slipped over her ankle, then glided slowly, effortlessly up her calf. She glared at Rafe, but he continued furiously scribbling meeting notes, not giving the least indication that he was feeling her up under the table. No wonder the man kept occupying her mind, despite the fact that she was living a nightmare. No one else on earth could have done it but this somewhat irritating, dreamy, dark-haired, six-foot-tall, solid hunk of a man.

Nevertheless, if she was honest, she felt like shattered glass inside. And just as determined to keep her smile firmly fixed in place. Last night, she hadn't gotten all the information she needed, so she couldn't afford to tell Rafe the truth, not yet. Maintaining a rigid upper body posture, she lightly kicked him under the table.

The damnable man stroked back with his toes.

Kimmie gurgled loudly from the tabletop, wiggling under the confining strap of the carrier and waving G.G., but if the two visiting power-brokers noticed anything unusual about the meeting or Mackinley's provocative red dress, they wisely kept it to themselves.

Clearing her throat, Mackinley dusted doughnut powder from her fingertips and continued, "The K and R industry, that's short for kidnap and recovery, is a new business with a very private clientele, so whatever marketing your agency provides will need to reflect that. As you can imagine, we've thought long and hard about the wisdom of advertising our services."

Ignoring the baby and Rafe, the two women nodded, focusing entirely on Mackinley. Ann, the frosted blonde in the red suit, spread sketches across the table, then tapped one with a long red fingernail. "This is my favorite. But, as you can see, all our initial ideas are discreet."

"Discretion is good," said Mackinley, staring pointedly at Rafe.

"But they're only initial ideas—" Leslie brushed a fallen wisp of dark hair from her forehead. "What we're looking for is your input."

Feeling Rafe's toe graze her stocking-clad knee, Mackinley reached under the table and calmly removed it. "The sketches look great," she assured the woman. Despite the duress she was under, she'd helped prepare for the meeting, so she knew exactly what Ransom High Risk was hoping to accomplish, not that she felt particularly professional at the moment. Leaning to better view the sketches, she hiked the neckline of the dress only to feel the hem rise. She'd meant to run home and change this morning, but the trip to Central Park last night had been horrible, and she'd slept through Rafe's alarm. Even worse, the way Rafe had scrutinized her this morning made clear that he was beginning to suspect something was wrong.

Leslie followed Mackinley's gaze. "Our graphics really are subdued, don't you agree?"

More subdued than this dress, Leslie. Mackinley set three aside. "These are the best, I think."

"We'll encourage solicitation of insurance policies for top executives," Ann continued, "and approach the corporations with dark blue portfolios."

"Not black?" Mackinley knew that had been Rafe's choice.

"Navy's less likely to communicate subterfuge," assured Leslie. "You're an insurance agency. Just like Prudential, you're insuring human lives."

"And by portfolio," put in Ann, "we mean binder."

Rafe's toe trekked back down to Mackinley's ankle. "Binders?" she managed, her voice sounding strangled to her own ears. "Did you get that, Rafe? Are you paying attention?"

Rafe shot her an amused glance. "Yes, ma'am."

"Subliminally speaking," continued Leslie, "a closing binder communicates privacy."

"Privacy is a very good thing," Mackinley said sharply, glancing at Rafe again. He merely smiled back innocently, his toe stroking a sensitive patch at the top of her foot.

"Please," Mackinley managed. "Tell us more about your ideas." Leaning back as Ann continued the presentation, Mackinley sipped coffee, needing it. She needed Rafe, too. When his toes—so warm and playful and comforting—slipped away, Mackinley's heart tugged unexpectedly. Tears pushed at her eyes. How could nothing more than this—his kisses, his touches, his flirtation—be giving her enough fuel to run on?

She'd been on edge for so long, living with secrets and lies. And in addition to still reeling from her father's death last year, she felt solely responsible for making sure Oliver was returned. Regardless of how their marriage had failed him, she knew no child should grow up without a father. Glancing through the window, into the blustery, windy winter day, she pushed aside the questions that still haunted her: if she'd more actively pursued her career and friendships during the marriage, would Oliver still have lost interest? Was there something more she could have done to keep them together? To engage his interest in having a family? Wasn't Oliver's unhappiness his own responsibility?

There'd been no time to work through all this unfinished business before he was kidnapped, and ever since she'd grabbed fear by the horns and ridden it out. She'd never known she was so strong. Day after day, she put a face on for the world—for her family and now Rafe—pretending to feel all right. But only Rafe really made her smile.

Mackinley knew he'd help her now.

But she was going to print his database first, just in

case, even if last night had been unbearable. Since the kidnappers obviously had her banking information, Mackinley figured they might also recognize her car, so she'd cabbed to the zoo. If she was seen driving Rafe's Humvee, she feared the kidnappers would wonder where it came from and follow her.

It was nearly midnight when she'd entered the park—silently tiptoeing down the stone steps, one hand nestled in her handbag, her fingers curling around the gun. Branches brushed against the rickety iron stair rail, and she'd shivered from the cold, assuring herself that wind caused the rustling sounds. But she knew people were down there. Homeless men and women. Drug dealers. Rapists.

She'd grown up in New York City, so she knew better than to venture into Central Park at night. With each step, she'd tensed, ready to scream bloody murder and shoot any mugger who grabbed for the money; she'd steeled herself against the calculating eyes she felt watching her from the cold darkness. Over and over, she'd said these words like a mantra: *after this, they'll let Oliver come home. After this, they'll let Oliver come home.*

Now, still wondering what she'd say to Oliver if she ever did speak with him again, her eyes settled on their son. K.G., she thought. The name was growing on her, probably because it was Rafe's suggestion and Mackinley was starting to like Rafe so much. Seeing him with K.G. completely convinced her Rafe wasn't as insensitive as she'd initially thought. Instinctively, he'd known how much she'd missed the baby, and she suspected that was why Rafe had brought him to work. She'd never guessed she could miss anyone so much as her baby. And Kimmie—K.G.—she mentally corrected, was so enamored of Rafe that he hadn't even seemed traumatized by their separation. A lump formed in her throat, and she swallowed around it.

Her baby needed a father. For that reason she'd go to any lengths to get Oliver back.

If her own father were still alive, would her situation be any different? She still missed him so much. During his fight with cancer, she'd been in denial; she simply hadn't been able to imagine life without him. Now she realized that her parents' marriage had been so full of riches that her own marital failure had been doubly hard to confront. Why hadn't she and Oliver made it, the way her folks had?

Ignoring the thoughts, she just wished she hadn't fallen asleep while printing Rafe's database because that meant she'd have to return alone tonight. At about four o'clock, she'd awakened at the computer, given up and mindlessly pulled on a blue lace nightie she'd found in Rafe's drawer. As she slid between those welcoming black silk sheets, Rafe's male scent had surrounded her, haunting her.

Listening to Ann and Leslie, who were still giving their presentation, Mackinley glanced toward the interior window overlooking the cubicles where the negotiators were pretending to confer. Really, they were amusing themselves by watching Rafe take meeting notes. Silencer sent her a ghostly smile, and when he raised his hand to wave, the too-short sleeve of a mottled brown suit rose almost to his elbow. Today Shark was wearing a shiny blue suit that made him look like a badly paid mob lawyer from the movies. Magnum's outfit was worse, since he was color-blind, and although Jack's navy suit and red, white and blue tie were well-fitting, his ex-military bearing, along with his stocky, scarred body, made him look like America's most patriotic hit man.

Mackinley felt her heart squeeze with maternal emotion she usually reserved for her son. So much for the new dress code, she thought. The womenless men who made up Ransom High Risk Negotiations definitely needed more than the average shot in the arm when it came to female attention.

Even Rafe. Not that he didn't look gorgeous—his suit's tasteful gray fabric accented his olive-toned skin and black hair and was woven with muted flecks of green that enhanced his green eyes, but the way he'd responded to her mom during dinner last night told Mackinley that Jack was right. Rafe had always missed having a mother.

"That would be your final estimate?" Rafe suddenly asked Ann, lifting those luscious, black-fringed green eyes from his notes. Forcing her attention on the meeting again, Mackinley frowned; K.G.'s flailing arms were swinging dangerously close to the mint bowl.

"It is," Ann said. "But you might consider discreet radio spots in the New York and D.C. areas. Or letting us design a website."

"It's a lot to take in," Mackinley said. "Once Rafe types the minutes I'll look them over, and then I'll discuss them with Jack Ransom, the president of the agency. As soon as I can, I'll get back to you with our final determination."

Pausing to humor K.G., who was now rambunctiously beating G.G. against the side of the carrier, Rafe began organizing papers on the table.

Ann sized him up. "That man's good," she said to Mackinley.

Despite all she'd been through in the past twelve hours, Mackinley managed a benevolent smile. "And he types seventy."

"Really?" Leslie sounded impressed. "Where did you find him? A headhunter?"

"The Francesca agency. It's a modeling agency," Mackinley couldn't help but add, biting back a smile at the faintly bemused curl of Rafe's lips.

"What was he modeling?" asked Ann.

"Mostly underwear," Mackinley said with a straight face. "You know, a designer line of wildly printed bikinis for men. Although I think he got a recent offer to do a commercial, didn't you, Rafe? Wasn't it for Grecian Formula haircolor? Or wearing one of those gauze outfits for Big Boss Sneakers?"

Rafe looked as if he wanted to throttle her. "Gillette razors," he said curtly, pushing his hair back from his forehead with a swipe of his hand.

"Oh," Mackinley murmured. "I knew it was some kind of...man thing." She smiled pleasantly at Ann and Leslie. "I love my people to have other interests," she explained. "And Rafe's the type who does all the little things without complaint."

"The little things?" Leslie echoed.

"Oh, you know—" Mackinley suddenly gasped. "Kimmie," she whispered in horror as his fist caught the mint bowl. He wasn't hurt, but the glass bowl rolled from the table to a chair before Mackinley could catch it. It didn't break, but tiny mints flew every which way.

"Allow me, ladies," Rafe said calmly. His head dipped under the paper tablecloth. His huge shoulders followed, vanishing. After a second, soft clinks sounded from under the table as Rafe dropped mints back into the bowl.

Loosening up, Ann chuckled and leaned across the table to grasp one K.G.'s hands. Her voice softened. "I guess this would qualify as one of Rafe's little things."

"He does," said Mackinley, feeling a strange stab of pain because the women didn't realize K.G. was hers. The feeling lingered, and suddenly, she thought about sharing the baby with a man like Rafe; it seemed easy to imagine people calling him daddy. Wasn't that what Mackinley had always wanted, after all? A responsive man who'd be proud to play papa? Clearing her voice, she continued, "What I meant was that Rafe sharpens pencils, fixes coffee..."

"What talent," declared Leslie generously.

"And Rafe's Spanish is fluent," added Mackinley.

Ann was stunned. "He's college educated?"

"Yes. Knowledgeable about a wide variety of subjects," Mackinley said graciously. And then her heart tripped inside her chest. Because under the table, two big, warm hands settled on her knees, and as they gently tried to part them, the hem of her dress rose to the tops of her thighs. Rafe Ransom, she supposed, had just decided to remind her who was boss. "Very knowledgeable," she managed, her voice rising as she tried to squeeze her knees back together. "Way *too* knowledgeable."

RAFE'S CHESTY, rumbling laugh reverberated through his spacious office as he closed the door. "You sure ended that meeting in a hurry." He settled his green eyes smokily on hers as he punched in the door lock, crossed to the window and made the blinds drop with a flick of his wrist. "Were you in a hurry to get somewhere?"

"Away from you?" Mackinley suggested sweetly.

Out of the corner of his eye, Rafe saw his computer screen go blank right as she began circling his black lacquer desk. He followed, stopping in front of her as she leaned against it, crossing her arms. "If you were really that hot to get away from me," he taunted softly, trapping her with his body, "I would have thought you'd move a lot faster, Mackinley."

"Next time I'll move like greased lightning," she promised.

"Glad you said 'next time.'" Rafe chuckled, pressing his hard muscled thighs between her softer, slimmer ones, inserting himself where he'd wanted to be since last night. "This time, I want you to keep moving real slow."

"You can't always get what you want."

"Not always. But today I will." He settled his hands on her waist, gently rubbing the inward dip, and he was glad when her slender arms decided to rise and circle his neck.

"Where's Kimmie?" she murmured.

"K.G.," Rafe corrected. He smiled as her palms turned warm and slightly damp on his nape, and as he gazed into her eyes he realized he liked the fact that he'd named her child; he wanted her to acknowledge it. "K.G.," he said again. "You really like it?"

"Yeah." There was no mistaking the soft catch in her voice. "I really do. I think it'll stick."

Rafe smiled. "Don't worry. He's in Dad's office, getting more attention than a movie star. Which means we're alone."

Slight color touched her cheeks. "Are we?"

"Very," Rafe murmured, roughening her neck with his mouth and chin, then kissing an earlobe.

"We'd better put the blinds back up, Rafe."

He traced the shell-like curve of her ear with his tongue. "But then people will see us."

"Exactly. And you were incorrigible in the meeting," she continued, her attempt at a schoolmarm's voice holding a dreamy lack of conviction that made him grin as he tilted back her head and drizzled slow, wet, lazy kisses down her neck. He couldn't get enough of her creamy skin, but he knew if he kept this up, he'd leave little bite marks. She sighed, saying, "What do you think you're doing?"

"You mean besides locking the door so I can kiss you?"

"Rafe," she reminded again. "We're in the office."

"True. But when it comes to you, Mackinley, I'm not feeling very particular about locations." Before she could protest, he lifted her to the desk, then he edged closer, his wide, caressing hands curling over the tops of her thighs, urging her legs around his waist. Feeling them lock behind his back, Rafe let his heated gaze burn down each inch of her, landing where the vampy red hemline stretched taut across her thighs. Gliding his hands upward, he worked his thumbs inward and rubbed slow circles. "You're gorgeous," he whispered, a swift shaft of heat lancing through him. In the stripes of winter sunlight seeping through the slats of the blinds, he could see Mackinley's cheeks darken, flushing with warmth.

"In the meeting, I was hardly going to let you..."

"No, you weren't going to let me do that." Under the table, she'd locked her knees together like the world's two strongest magnets. "But you wanted me to touch you there, didn't you, Mackinley?"

Her eyes widened, but she didn't deny it. She swallowed hard, the pulse in her throat ticking wildly, passion darkening her eyes, deepening the gold and red flecks. The sound of her low voice shuddered through him. "We're at work."

"Then I'd better start working." Locking his mouth to hers, he kissed her hard and deep, arching to her female heat, feeling her through his slacks as his tongue traced and parted her lips, plunging between them.

Leaning back, she shivered. "You call that work?"

He suddenly frowned, despite how much she'd aroused him. Instead of answering, he said, "You look so tired. Are you sure my place was okay?"

Her lips were wet from his, glistening. "It was fine."

"I don't think so." His chest tightened, his breath turning shallow. He was hard, nestled where he needed her most, and he wanted to be inside her. Now. He shuddered again, imagining how she might feel around him, so hot and sweet. But he was more concerned about whatever she was hiding. "Something's wrong. Something kept you up last night."

"Fantasies about you?" she suggested.

He shot her a long, contemptuous glance. "Playing to my male vanity?"

"Are you vain?"

"No." Somehow he refrained from slanting his mouth across hers and hungrily claiming her lips again, even though he craved the taste of her—all morning coffee, doughnuts and mints. He knew her open mouth was still hot from the kisses they'd shared; hot, too, from the memories of yesterday's kisses, but he said, "C'mon, Mackinley. Talk to me."

"About what?"

She was acting so innocent that he had no choice but to seduce her into talking. "About kissing you." His breath caught and this time, when he gave in and kissed her, he splayed a broad hand over her rib cage, feeling the quickening rise and fall of her chest. Gliding his hand up he felt her tense—and he wanted that. He wanted her to anticipate the palm that now slowly slid over her breast. Brushing a tight bud with his knuckles, he murmured, "So tiny, so tight," then unable to stop himself, no longer caring where they were, Rafe did what he'd fantasized about for days and slipped his hand under her neckline, inside her bra. Releasing a chesty groan, he pushed down the stretchy fabric. Elastic caught beneath her breast, lifting her as he urged out her flesh.

The instant he saw her, he forgot his worry over her sleeplessness. Without even trying she'd reduced him to his fundamental essence: male. "I need to see you," Rafe gasped hoarsely, gazing down where the sloping silken skin of her uncovered breast was as pale as winter sunlight. When his eyes caught hers, he knew this necessarily quick, stolen moment could never be enough to satisfy either of them. They needed so much more. They needed to be alone and naked, fully joined.

But that was later.

And this was now. Unmasked need radiated from her eyes, and since they didn't have much time, he leaned and gently claimed her with his searing mouth. As he suckled, she whimpered and he answered silently, rolling his hips, letting her feel his length and heat where she wanted him most. He could barely believe this was happening. Somehow, she'd engaged his emotions, and he wished it wasn't too early to tell her how he felt...that she was the kind of woman about whom he could get serious.

"Rafe, we can't do this," she whispered.

"We already are," he murmured as her hands slid into his hair, her blunt-tipped fingers massaging his scalp.

Her voice was low, hoarse. "Somebody could come in here."

As if on cue, a rap sounded at the door. "Rafe?"

Damn. It was Shark. Rafe blew out a sigh. "Be out in a minute," he called, his whole body burning up with want. "I'm, uh, taking dictation with Mackinley." Lowering his voice, he righted Mackinley's neckline. "Don't worry. The door's locked. I promise." Rafe stepped back, feeling strangely shaken.

"Maybe we can stay together tonight," she murmured.

His voice was so rough he didn't even recognize it. "Good idea, Mackinley."

She looked very well kissed, and her voice was huskier than usual, almost lulling. "I've got a lot of good ideas," she promised with a smile.

He smiled back. "I'll bet you do." Reaching, he trailed a finger down her cheek as he recalled all she'd said last night, in the foyer of her building. "Mackinley..."

Uncertain emotion was in her eyes. "Hmm?"

Last night, he was sure she'd been trying to say she wanted to sleep with him and that she feared being used, but he didn't know her well enough to talk openly. He searched for the words. "I like you," he finally said. "That's all."

Stretching on tiptoe, she pressed a sweet, almost chaste, minty kiss to his mouth that affected him more than all the others combined. "I like you, too." She paused, those incredibly soft, secretive brown eyes flickering over his face, making him feel warm, wanted. Rafe wondered if true love could begin this way. Her eyes said she was wondering the same, but aloud she said, "You'd better see what Shark wants."

Rafe nodded. After another brief kiss, he turned and strode toward the door. He was standing there, his hand on the knob, his back to Mackinley when, for the first time in twenty-four hours, he came to his senses and everything suddenly snapped into place.

Rafe was a professional, so he didn't turn around. But the cell phone Mackinley always carried was on his desk. He'd also just realized that the document open on his computer screen when he'd entered the room required his private passcode, which meant Mackinley had broken into his system. Every niggling thing that had bothered him for the past two weeks resurfaced, as well as Barbara's nervousness last night, Mackinley's sleeplessness and the family's noticeably diminished resources. Mackinley was driving to work, too, and in Rafe's experience, one reason for having a vehicle in Manhattan was quick transport, to deliver ransom payments. Most likely, she carried the cell phone for reasons having nothing to do with her baby.

If she hadn't blinded him with lust, Rafe would have recognized all the warning signs. Now his own stupidity made him seethe. Someone close to the Leighs had obviously been kidnapped.

"Rafe?"

"On my way out," he answered. Feeling furious, he slowly turned the knob and walked out the door.

"RAFE," BARBARA called through the doorway. "Are you sure you're all right, dear?"

"I just need to lie down for a minute." Rafe tried to sound sick as he sent a piercing glare around Mackinley's cramped little closet of a bedroom. "It's just a headache..."

"Are you sure some ibuprofen wouldn't help?"

Rafe's eyes landed on K.G., who was watching him curiously from the crib. "No, but thanks for asking."

"Are you sure I can't take Kimmie?"

"No, I'm enjoying his company."

Hearing Barbara's footsteps recede, Rafe went back to searching Mackinley's drawers. Eventually, he'd find something. He always did. So far, Rafe was assuming her father, Carter Leigh, wasn't really dead and was being held for ransom. "Especially now that I know who he is." Rafe had found a phone listing for the Leighs' previous address on Jane Street in the West Village, and he'd found out that Carter Leigh was *the* Carter Leigh, of the Leigh Corporation. The steel company wasn't global and Leigh had taken the company public years ago and eventually gotten out of the business, but he was definitely worth more than the average Joe.

"So, why didn't she tell me?" More than anything, that infuriated Rafe. What was between them physically was so right that it should have invited confidences. He was an honorable guy. He helped people for a living. Why the hell hadn't Mackinley trusted him with the truth?

There was only one answer. She'd been blatently using him.

Chewing the inside of his cheek, Rafe suddenly realized he'd quit rifling through the drawer. Staring down at the plain cotton panties in his hand made him recall holding her. Today in the office, she'd felt so sweet against him, her head curled into his shoulder, her golden cap of hair feeling like pure silk on his chin. Now his chest constricted with uncharacteristic emotion, his loins tightened.

And he got madder.

While she'd been pressing that sweet, chaste kiss to his lips, she'd been well aware she was insinuating herself into his life under false pretenses. It was the only reasonable conclusion, and it explained why someone with her education would work for such low pay, not to mention why someone so sweet would bother to seduce him. The facts should have doused his passion like ice on a fire.

But they didn't.

He wanted her more than ever. He'd even considered sleeping with her before blowing her cover, but he unfortunately had more integrity than that. "Even if she doesn't think so," he muttered. It had cost him to send her packing tonight. They'd had dinner at her apartment again, and then he and K.G. had kissed her goodbye at the door. She didn't ask him to spend the night, of course. "Probably because she's printing information from my database." He'd only known her two weeks, but now he could read her like a book.

Realizing he was still standing there like a fool, holding her panties, he tossed them back into the drawer and stripped her bed. Lifting the flimsy mattress with one hand, he checked beneath, then he wiggled under the bed until his massive shoulders got stuck. After that, he looked behind her few framed prints, then through photographs of her family. For a long time, he stared at a picture of her in diapers.

"Cute," he finally muttered, as much as he hated admitting it. "But she's just like Charmaine," he added. "Using me to get her out of a jam."

And then he tossed aside the photograph and ripped her closet apart.

He found the papers he sought well hidden on a closet shelf. "It figures," he grumbled, tossing them onto the bed and staring down at some newspaper pictures of himself. One grainy black and white showed him striding across blacktop, carrying toddlers from a school bus; in another, he was outside a Manhattan bank. So, Mackinley knew about those jobs.

"And about Brussels." Two years ago, a disgruntled ex-employee had taken over a corporate headquarters, and Rafe had negotiated the release of his coworkers. Mackinley had even unearthed a reference to a love-obsessed student who'd grabbed a diplomat's daughter in Cairo. Rafe's clients were often private people, so he'd always stayed out of the papers—at least until he'd reversed policy and decided to advertise.

"I can't believe it." She'd found every existing reference to the agency, which was why she'd come knocking.

Fishing out a manilla envelope, he schooled himself not to react as he opened the clasp, sliding out some Polaroid photographs. At least she'd had the common sense to bag them in transparent plastic, in case there were prints, not that Rafe was in the mood to praise her street savvy. He studied the subject of the photos—a good-looking blond male, but too young to be Carter Leigh.

Rafe scrutinized each photo. In each, the man was holding up a Spanish-language newspaper, and judging from the length of his hair, he'd been in captivity awhile. He looked tired and grimy, and Rafe noted that he was wearing round, wire-framed glasses. Glasses often got lost, or were crunched underfoot while a victim was shoved into a vehicle, but not always.

Who was he, though?

Since the Leighs' family pictures hadn't included siblings, Rafe had assumed Mackinley was an only child. But maybe this was a brother. "It fits," Rafe said. Maybe he was bad news, disinherited. "Maybe he headed down to South America, was slumming around and got into drugs."

But that was only conjecture. There was only one way to find out the truth—if Mackinley Leigh was even capable of telling the truth. As he shoved the papers into a modified inside pocket of his overcoat, preparing to pay her a visit, Rafe assured himself this was pure business. The woman had infiltrated Ransom High Risk, and Rafe's anger had absolutely nothing to do with the fact that she'd played him for a fool.

5

RAFE'S MASSIVE shoulders crowded the doorway, and a shaft of light from the living room illuminated his furious features.

"You scared me!" Mackinley exclaimed, grabbing the neckline of the powder blue lace nightie she'd borrowed as she hopped up from where she'd been crouched near the head of Rafe's bed. Moments before, she'd been lying between the black silk sheets, drifting and missing K.G. and her mom and worrying about Oliver, when she realized someone else was in the apartment. Now she had half a mind to say that Rafe would never know how lucky he was; she'd been heading for her gun.

Not that he sounded particularly concerned. His voice was deceptively soft. "Scared you?"

Her heart was still pounding. Of course he had. The instant she'd heard footsteps, she'd sat bolt upright, illogically believing the kidnappers had come for her, or that Oliver was being returned. "Rafe," she said, her calm tone hiding the rapid-fire thoughts about his intrusion. "You can't come barging into a New York City apartment without using the intercom."

"I just did." Parting the sides of his overcoat, he shoved his hands deep into the pockets of threadbare black jeans while his glowering, assessing green eyes danced around the room. After a moment, they lanced into her again, as coldly dangerous as shards of ice.

Her heart suddenly pulling, Mackinley wished she could tell him that, for months, the netherworld between waking and dreams had been filled with ill omens for her, but she knew she was only motivated by wanting his compassion, and that wasn't fair, not when she was using him in such a horrible, calculated way. "You really did scare me," she repeated.

"You'll live."

If I'm lucky. As she became more awake, her mind registered the fact that Rafe had hardly come home with seduction on his mind. Her eyes flicked over him. Nope. No flowers bunched in his fist, no bottle of bubbly and a corkscrew. Even in the darkness, she could feel the intensity of his eyes, the violence of the gesture as he pushed back his windblown hair. Realizing he'd rushed here impulsively, she felt her heart sink; he must have found something incriminating at her place. But what? He'd never have found her file on Ransom High Risk unless he felt he had reason to search. Had her mother broken down and told him the truth about Oliver? Mackinley decided to let Rafe do the talking. "Uh...why didn't you call?"

"This is my apartment. I hardly need an invitation."

"True," she admitted, wishing he wasn't looking around as if she was robbing him blind. Which, of course, she was. Glancing toward where the printer was spitting out continuous-feed paper, she wondered how to divert his attention, then she swallowed guiltily, her eyes straying to his mouth while her mind recalled its warmth. As much as she was craving the heated crush of his lips, she still had to negotiate Oliver's release and the database printout might help. Somehow, she had to grab it and run, especially since she had the distinct impression seducing Rafe was out of the question at the moment. Over the hum of the printer, she mustered what she hoped would pass for an accusing tone, to throw Rafe off the scent of her wrongdoing. "Rafe, really," she managed, her voice rising righteously, "you owe me an apology. You could have been anybody. A rapist or a mugger..."

His lush mouth curled in displeasure. Dryly, he asked, "You think I look like a rapist, Mackinley?"

"Well, no," she admitted. "No, of course not. But I didn't know what to do. I thought somebody was breaking in."

Anger now seemed to be radiating from every controlled male inch of him. "Well, you thought right. Somebody did."

Meaning her. She tried to look offended at the accusation, but it was difficult when she'd been caught with her hand in the cookie jar.

He added, "And I'm beginning to think you'd know exactly what to do."

He'd definitely found something in her apartment. She winced. Should she pretend she intended to file copies of the database material at the Ransom High Risk office? Besides, maybe she was wrong and Rafe would believe she was really doing extra work, since his father was paying overtime. She nodded toward the printer, deciding to take the middle ground. "I can explain."

"Feel free."

Now she was stuck. "You mean right now?"

"Yeah. Right now, Mackinley."

As she continued considering her options—any number of lies versus the not-so-simple truth—Rafe's gaze shifted to where she'd closed the heavy drapes against the cold, starry, velvet night. She felt a moment's relief until those penetrating eyes returned, now burning down every pale, exposed inch of her skin. Not that her scanty outfit seemed to change his mood for the better. Even worse, his long brooding silences were increasing her nervousness. Deciding defense was still the best offense, she finally mustered an acid tone, "Obviously something prompted this little intrusion, Rafe, so why don't you simply tell me what?"

He merely stood there staring at her, as if unable to believe her gross deception. Despite the room's darkness, Mackinley could feel him sizing her up. Like it or not she'd now become Rafe Ransom's adversary, and only when a pang of hurt registered did she realize she still wanted his comfort, not his anger. Oh, well. So much for hoping his broad shoulders might share the burden of her ordeal, that maybe he'd help her make the drop when the kidnappers called again, demanding the extra ten thousand she'd been told to get.

Another thought suddenly occurred to her. What if she wasn't using Rafe, after all? What if she was really starting to fall for him? Her heart missing a dangerous beat, she told herself Rafe belonged with women like Charmaine—exciting, daring types who stared down from billboards, dramatically draped in gauze. Women who'd leave him, or whom he could easily leave, since—as everyone at the office so regularly pointed out—Rafe was definitely not the marrying kind. Yes, he'd probably been fooling himself when he was thinking of settling down with Charmaine.

"First," Rafe finally began with a softness of voice that Mackinley feared indicated concealed murderous fury, "I know your father, Carter Leigh, is the guy who owned the Leigh Corporation, right? He's the steel manufacturer?"

Forcing her thoughts away from Rafe's ex-girlfriend, she anxiously finger-combed the waves of her sleep-tousled hair and tucked it behind her ears. "Dad *was*. He sold the company years ago."

"When exactly?"

That information was beside the point, and Mackinley suspected Rafe was biding time, trying to make her squirm. Didn't their shared kisses mean anything? Hadn't they made him warm to her? Was he really mad about whatever he'd found? "I don't know what's made you so mad, but if you intend to interrogate me," she managed coolly, determined not to let him see her sweat but knowing he had the upper hand, "do you mind if I get a robe?"

"As a matter of fact I do."

She shifted from one bare foot to the other, glancing toward the rumpled silk sheets that probably still held her body warmth. So much for required bed rest. "I'm nearly naked."

"Really? Then I guess our evening just got a little more interesting." Rafe reached for the switch beside the bedroom door and snapped on the overhead light.

Great. Rapidly blinking to adjust her eyes, Mackinley became doubly aware of her attire—and of how Rafe's husky rumble of a voice had been stirring her blood. Instinctively, she crossed her arms, but the movement only lifted her breasts and accentuated the cleavage, drawing Rafe's attention to where chilled flesh spilled from the scooped lace neckline. It wasn't a good time to register the coldness of the room—or that she was still experiencing stabs of jealousy over Charmaine. Could she help it if *she* wasn't a model? Feeling Rafe's seemingly casual perusal, heat rose on her cheeks. "Seen enough yet?"

He considered a long moment. "No."

The one word was packed with dark emotion and rough, edgy sexuality. Not that she'd shrink like a hothouse flower just because Rafe Ransom was in a foul temper, but Shark's ex-girlfriend's nightie was dangerously sexy, like nothing Mackinley owned unless she counted the comparatively tame white teddies she'd bought after she'd realized she was pregnant. Not that Oliver had responded.

Rafe did, though, and as Mackinley acknowledged that fact, she felt a sudden, sweet rush of yearning. Rafe's massive chest rose and fell dramatically, as if he were trying to get control of himself. He glanced at the printer again and said, "Start explaining."

She couldn't help but say, "I will if you'll stop staring."

"Don't worry. You're safe. You're really not affecting me all that much."

"I didn't say I was." She'd assumed Rafe hadn't pushed to stay with her tonight because he'd changed his mind about wanting her sexually, but now she wasn't sure. Edging along the mattress, toward the foot of the bed, she wondered how she could get around Rafe and into the living room, where her robe was. "Rafe, this is totally inhumane. Just let me get my robe."

"Not before I get some answers."

Righteous indignation welled within her, since she was the true victim here, but it faltered when her eyes accidently dipped over Rafe. His black jeans had faded to gray and their soft, glovelike fit cupped his powerfully firm male contours. Where his hands had disappeared into his pockets, she could see the ridges of knuckles and another traitorously delicious shiver slid down her spine as she remembered those hands— their broadness, their darkness, how they gently stroked her cheek today after he'd kissed her.

His voice was hard to read; it was part challenge, part amusement, but all seductive hoarse male whisper. "Who's staring now, Mackinley?"

She'd wanted to divert *his* attention, not her own. "As I was trying to say, if you'd just be nice and let me get my robe..."

"Spare me the dramatics."

Easy for him to say. He wasn't the one who was half-naked. She exhaled a shaky sigh. "When my dad got sick, almost six years ago, he sold the family business and became an investor. Is that what you wanted me to say, Rafe?"

"The *business*? You make it sound like a family hardware store, Mackinley," he said, his voice laced with censure. "The Leigh Corporation was a national steel company."

"Was being the operative term."

Blowing out a murderous sigh, Rafe reached inside his coat, and her eyes widened as he yanked her research materials from an inside pocket. She should have known. "You found them," she murmured as he shrugged out of the coat and flung it into the armchair. Beneath his tight white T-shirt, she could make out a matt of thick black tangled hair; squashed beneath his shirt, it looked like a small dark forest that had been flattened by a steamroller. Her eyes shifted to the circle of tattooed leaves wrapping his biceps, then to where his strong ropy forearm quivered with smaller muscles as he held up the fistful of newspapers.

"I see them," she told him.

Shooting her a disgusted look, he tossed them on top of his coat, his eyes drifting over her in a bold, if oddly disinterested caress that made her already boiling internal thermostat rise once more. Her face suddenly felt so hot that she was sure she could fry an egg on it. Suddenly she wished he'd yell, instead of exercising this annoying, unbelievable control. "You're enjoying this little game of yours, aren't you, Rafe?"

"Oh yeah," he said. "Having a blast, sweetheart."

Well, she hoped this little outfit drove him crazy. "No wonder you didn't want to come here tonight," she couldn't help but say, still feeling concerned about his lack of trying. "You were obviously too busy violating my home, searching my room."

"I don't remember you issuing any invitations." Rafe stared pointedly at the computer. "I guess you were too busy with your own...uh, violations."

She'd about had it. "I wanted your help, Rafe! You've no idea what I've been dealing with!"

When his molten eyes dropped over her again they turned as hot as searchlights. "Right," he muttered. "You wanted my help, and you were willing to do absolutely anything to get it, weren't you Mackinley?"

A tight knot of fury coiled inside her. "What's *that* supposed to mean?"

"You know what it means."

Her jaw dropped. "You don't think I..."

"Tried to seduce me because you wanted my help? Sure I do."

He knew her better than that. "Bastard." She tossed off the word, trying to goad him.

"You have no idea what a bastard I can be."

He was implying she was about to find out. Well, no matter what Rafe said, she'd never let him know how much he'd gotten to her in the past twenty-four hours. She shrugged. "I was beginning to think you might be a nice guy."

"Am I supposed to feel guilty?"

"Yes."

"Well I don't. Besides, you obviously researched me well enough to know exactly who I am."

She had. She'd known about his military background and about some of his father's shadier dealings. It was probably why the second Rafe's strong arms had enveloped her in warmth, she'd breathed easily for the first time in months.

He thrust back his midnight hair, jabbing his thick fingers through the strands, then he nodded curtly toward the chair. "So if that's not your father, who is it?"

Her heart hammered harder. "You thought my father..."

Rafe shrugged. "I thought you might have lied about him being dead. I thought maybe he'd been kidnapped."

Her heart wrenched, renewed grief over the loss opening like a barely sutured wound. "No, my dad's really dead." Rapidly, she blinked her eyes, holding back tears. "I wish he wasn't."

Rafe's gaze softened, but only for an instant. "So, who's this?"

"My husband."

"Your *what!*" Rafe's damning eyes—so smoky, green and penetrating—pierced right through her.

"My husband."

Rafe looked as if he'd never trust her again. "I thought you were divorced?"

"I am."

"*Ex*-husband, then?"

"Yes." She was getting tired of Rafe's tone and how his raw sexuality made her feel so jittery. "Anyway, it doesn't matter. You don't care." Even as she said the words, she knew she wanted him to deny them. When he didn't, she continued, "Now, if you'll just let me get dressed, I'll be on my way."

"I don't think so."

She'd been afraid it wouldn't be that easy. "What do you want?" Fighting a shiver, she realized he could probably call the authorities. He'd given her keys to the apartment, but he'd hardly authorized her to steal information.

"You're really divorced?"

As if he didn't believe her. "Yes. Satisfied now?"

There was no mistaking the fact that his eyes were busy, steamily tracing the sloping mounds of her breasts. "No," he murmured, as if he couldn't help himself. "Where you're concerned, I don't think I'd ever be satisfied." He left her to imagine what exactly would satisfy him, and continued, his voice turning huskier, almost lazy, "If you're divorced, why do you want him back?"

She gaped at Rafe. "Because Oliver's...a human being. And the father of my son. Of *K.G.*" She emphasized the name Rafe had given her baby.

"K.G.," Rafe murmured, and she could swear she saw raw emotion flicker in his eyes. "Is that all?"

"What do you mean? Wanting my son to have a father isn't enough?" Unexpected venom shot through her, and it felt good—like an antidote to her inescapable, unwanted, persistent attraction to Rafe. At least until she realized that Rafe looked oddly vulnerable.

He said, "Do you love him?"

Her breath caught and her heart squeezed almost painfully tight. It was exactly what she'd asked about Charmaine. What if she was wrong? What if Rafe had started to care about her? He had dated a lot of women—she knew that—but was Rafe as affected as she by the proximity they'd shared in the past twenty-four hours? Was he mad because he thought she still loved Oliver? Was he jealous? Could only a few kisses turn a man's head that much? "Oliver and I are divorced," she repeated.

"That doesn't answer my question."

"No," she said. "I'm a failure at marriage, okay?"

"Who said you're a failure?"

"Oliver." She shrugged. "I...I guess I do want another chance to talk to him about what went wrong in our marriage, if he's ever released...." As she said the words, Rafe's gaze darkened, so she rushed on. "I took the job as your assistant because I needed help," she began, then she told him the whole story. "But when you came back to town, after your father hired me, you weren't very approachable. I asked you about charity cases, but you said you never took them." Feeling distracted, she lifted a hand and began chewing the skin around an index finger.

His voice was testy. "Don't do that."

"What?"

"Bite your nails."

She crossed her arms over her chest again. "Obviously, you wouldn't help me unless..."

His anger was back, and she steeled herself against his soft insinuating taunt. "Unless you gave me a little encouragement?"

It was true she'd thought about seducing him... right down to the last details. In fact, she was still thinking about it. "What choice did I have?" she protested. "How else *could* I get through to you?"

His voice was strangely gruff. "I respond to things other than sex."

Such as? she wondered. Didn't he know how vulnerable she felt, standing here in an outfit made for seduction with every inch of her body laid bare for his hungry eyes? Bushy black eyebrows and a thick fringe of jet eyelashes framed those eyes, and right now they looked so green and interested in her physical being that her heart fluttered. "That's not how it seemed last night."

His football player's body was still tensely controlled, every muscle coiled like a spring. "Really?" His voice lowered, turning almost silky. "How did it seem?"

Nice. He'd was so easy to be with—thoughtful, attentive, kind. But she wasn't about to admit that right now. "Do you really expect some verbal confirmation of how you affected me?"

"No."

But he did. She was suddenly sure of it. He was well aware she was printing the database materials, but he seemed angrier about her fledgling seduction. Why? What was going on in his mind?

He drummed his fingers against his thigh. "How long's your ex been gone?"

"Nine months."

Expelling another long, drawn-out sigh, Rafe stared at her so long that her mind strayed, and she had to fight intrusive thoughts about the hot feel of his mouth and the slow suggestive way he kissed.

"Nine *months?*" he finally repeated softly.

Mackinley nodded. She'd never known how she'd survived. "As you can see," she suddenly couldn't help but say, angered because she had a suspicion he was going to deny his attraction, "I've had to steel myself against worse fates than you, Rafe."

"Sleeping with me would have been pure hell, I'm sure," he returned wryly.

No. She'd wanted that since she'd first seen him. "I'm out of money, out of time, out of hope," she forced herself to say. "But don't worry, Rafe. I'm not begging for help. You made it quite clear you don't take charity cases. Still...if you must know, Oliver's been gone since right after the baby was born. He's never even seen his son."

Rafe looked none too happy. "He's been gone that long?"

Panic made her stomach muscles clench. "Is that...bad?"

Rafe uttered a soft, sarcastic sound that wasn't particularly promising. "You mean worse than getting kidnapped in general, Mackinley?"

She didn't know what to say to that. "Yes. I guess."

Shrugging, he blew out another exasperated breath. "Depends."

She couldn't keep her voice steady. "On what?"

"Just about everything. Have you made payments?"

"Four."

"Four!" he exploded.

Before she could respond, he turned abruptly on his heel, strode into the living room and returned with her robe. He came all the way into the room, almost to the bed. Balling the robe, he threw it, and she caught it against her stomach, her lips parting in protest. It was the sudden violence of the action that made her decide to tell him the truth. "Rafe, I know what you're thinking." She swallowed hard. "Or at least I *think* I know. But I didn't come on to you to get information." Maybe she was a fool for saying it, but no matter what happened now, she didn't want him to think it. She squinted, searching for a reaction. "Rafe?"

He held up a staying hand. "Please."

"I...don't want you to think I'm a..." Glancing away, she settled on, "...a slut."

"You?" His harsh, choked, self-recriminating laugh made clear he thought he'd somehow debased her. "I admit it," he said. "I was mad as hell when I found those papers. But I knew it didn't make sense that you'd come on to me like that."

Her heartbeat was too fast, running like a wild thing, and she couldn't move. She wanted to protest, but she couldn't find the right words. "What?" she finally croaked. "Do you think..." She couldn't force herself to say it.

He raised an eyebrow. "Think you're too good for me?"

"Is that what you think?"

"Probably."

Rafe Ransom was voicing insecurity? She couldn't believe it. "Well, I'm not," she managed, words she knew she'd regret gushing forth. "You're so...so much nicer than I thought, Rafe. You wished me Happy Valentine's Day yesterday, and brought Kimmie—I mean, K.G.—to work today, and you're so indulgent with my mother...." Her voice trailed off.

"Mackinley, you're..."

Her breath caught as she waited, watching him thrust his fingers distractedly into his hair again. He looked so strangely disheveled, as if he'd come here driven by pure male emotion, and now she felt a small smile tug at her lips. "I'm?"

"Too trusting. Gullible. And in need of help," he bit out. "So, do me a favor, just get dressed and get your things."

It was hardly what she'd been hoping for. "But, Rafe, I..."

"Please don't explain. I'll wait in the other room." But he didn't move. His eyes were on her barely covered breasts now, and when her gaze dipped, there was no mistaking how her scanty attire had affected him. His soft worn jeans bulged, and her eyes followed the curve of the zipper before darting to his face. His throat worked visibly as he swallowed. "Get dressed, sweetheart," he repeated hoarsely. "Please."

"Why? Where are we going?"

He muttered something unintelligible, but she thought he said, "To bed if you don't get some clothes on." Raising his voice, he said, "You shouldn't be here, in case anybody's following you. Besides, they could have followed me. They probably don't know who I am, but it would be better for me to question you at your place. You need to be home with your baby, anyway. Your mother knows everything?"

Mackinley nodded, feeling so touched by his concern for K.G. that a lump lodged in her throat. "Not absolutely everything. But most of it." Her voice caught, and her heart squeezed almost painfully. "Are you thinking about helping us, Rafe?"

Emotion made his eyes glitter as if she'd attacked his personal code of honor. "What do you think, Mackinley?"

A soft whimper escaped her lips. For days, she'd battled it, but suddenly she was losing against the tears that were always about to fall. Dropping the balled-up robe on the bed, she staggered toward him.

He backed toward the door. Sounding oddly shaken, he said, "Mackinley, stay away. I'm begging you. Just get dressed."

Her raw throat affected her voice, turning it raspy. "Rafe. I told you. I meant to ask for help, but when you saw me, you didn't want me at the office. And when I asked you about taking charity cases, you said no. I would have come last month, when I first found out about the agency, but the people who have Oliver said they'd kill him—"

"Kill him?" Rafe echoed.

"Yes, they did. And I was scared. I'm still scared. I

read that involving authorities can make things even worse."

"Sometimes it can," Rafe admitted.

"But I'm out of money now. I can't pay you anything. Most of the money was electronically transferred. And last night, before I took the forty thousand to Central Park, they told me—"

Something in Rafe's eyes stopped her. He looked ready to explode again. "Forty *thousand?* As in dollars? Last *night?*"

"Don't worry," she added quickly, nodding toward the purse on the desk. "I had protection. I have a gun."

He looked fit to be tied. "A gun," he echoed, his blazing green eyes wide with disbelief as he crossed the room and began rifling through her bag, uninvited.

He swore as he unchambered the small twenty-two revolver, "Rafe," she whispered, peering at him. "Did I do something wrong?"

"Do you even know how to shoot this?"

"A man at the store told me what to do. Basically, you pop in the bullets, then unhinge the little thingy that covers the red dot. That's the safety. Then bingo, he said all you have to do is pull the trig—"

Something in his expression stopped her again. Very carefully setting aside the weapon, Rafe headed for the bed and simply sat down. "Central Park," he muttered venomously, punching the mattress with his clenched fist.

"That's where they told me to go," she said defensively.

"And you took a gun? You carried that much cash? On foot?"

"I didn't have a choice."

"You didn't even tell me? What kind of a bastard do you think I am?"

"I don't think you're a...a bastard, Rafe," Mackinley protested. "I just said that because I was mad." Stepping gingerly in front of him, she placed a hand lightly on his shoulder and peered down. This close, she could smell him, and his scent was so strong, so male that her breath quickened. Beneath her palm, his shoulder muscles suddenly quivered, and he glanced up sharply. His gaze was level with her breasts, and for a second, he didn't seem able to tear his eyes away. Staring down, she realized she didn't want him to. He looked almost desperate to touch her, and when he refrained she was tempted to guide his hand...

"Mackinley," he said on a slow exhalation of labored breath. "I've been working kidnapping jobs for years. I know what people go through. It's like torture. It's worse than being in prison. Besides your mother, have you told *anyone* about this?"

She shook her head. "Mom knows some things, but I've tried to protect her as much as I could. Since dad died..." She simply couldn't finish. Suddenly it was all too much. She'd been controlling her fear for everybody else's sake, and now Rafe suspected she'd used her body to get his help. "I admit it," she forced herself to say. "I came to your office with an agenda, but after you kissed me..."

His voice was almost rough. "What?"

The moment she said the words, she knew they were true. "Everything changed."

Looking positively sick, Rafe reached and caught her hand, turning it in his, laying her fingers on his palm. Smoothing them, he gently touched the ragged, bitten-down tips of her fingernails, then traced the worn, pink cuticles. "No wonder you've been so nervous."

"But having you around..." Her mouth turned dry. "I...feel a lot less scared."

He grimaced, as if berating himself for not reading her mind, and then she felt another big, warm hand, this time on her hip. Through the lace, she could feel throbbing pulses from his fingertips, and she was unable to stop an involuntary shiver.

"Cold?"

Gazing down at him, she slowly shook her head. "No." In fact, her whole body felt lusciously warm.

He shook his head ruefully. "So, at first, you were going to try to seduce me into helping you?"

She nodded. "At first."

"Well, it's a deal then," he said, his voice so low that she wondered if she was imagining the undercurrents of emotion. "But c'mere first." Gently, he guided her into his lap, and she settled against his groin while he smoothed her hair, coaxing her to curl her head on his chest. His voice lowered another notch. "Now tell me everything."

Instead, she merely whispered, "Rafe." And then she wrapped her arms around his neck and did what she'd never allowed herself to do during these horrible months—she wept.

"THANKS," MACKINLEY whispered later. Feeling a huge splayed hand slowly gliding down her spine, rubbing her back through the gown's lace, she curled her head against a hard pectoral and listened to the powerful beat of Rafe's heart. Against her cheek, his T-shirt was soft, but he smelled like sweat and muscle, the way a man should smell. Even though she was divorced, she suddenly felt traitorous; she wanted Rafe more than she had her husband, and if Rafe hadn't kissed her, she'd never have known.

"You okay?"

She nodded, squeezing a bicep. "Just feeling your muscles."

It obviously wasn't what he expected her to say. "Make you feel better?"

"Yes." She sighed. His strength was so comforting that she could have been listening to rain on a tin roof. She could almost hear the pinging drops; she thought of other such sounds, too—the hum of air conditioners on long hot summer nights, and of how strong winds whistled, tunneling down the avenues between skyscrapers. She didn't move, but she thought she felt Rafe's lips brush her hair, so lightly she could have imagined it. "Strange," she murmured, "but I feel like we're somewhere else, like a cabin in the woods."

"Not many cabins in Manhattan."

"No," she agreed.

After a long moment, he said, "I can't promise you anything. But I'll do whatever I can for you, Mackinley."

Emotion turned her throat raw again. Her bare legs were dangling between his parted thighs, and she swung them, snuggling, pressing her hip more comfortably into the cradle of his lap. Despite the cooling temperature of the room, she felt warm in his arms.

The printer had quit running, and everything was quiet now except for their rhythmic breathing and muted traffic sounds.

He sounded strangely uncertain. "Sure you're okay?"

Gazing up, Mackinley nodded. Surveying him, she thought of the lives he'd saved, and she wondered why she was so surprised to see his smoky green eyes holding so much compassion. Sliding her palm under his hair and around his neck, she cupped the nape, stroking gently with her thumb, enjoying the feel of his sleek black hair on the back of her hand. Before she thought better of it, she whispered, "Charmaine was a fool."

A slow, wry smile curled his lips. "If you had a choice between me and Big Boss Sneakers, who would you pick?"

"You."

His voice was husky. "Really?"

She nodded. "I wish this moment would never end."

"I can see why. You've been under a lot of stress."

That wasn't exactly what she'd meant. She wanted Rafe to know how much his presence anchored her. "I feel like I've found peace in a storm."

"Watch out," he warned. "It could be the eye of a hurricane."

Did Rafe mean their relationship or Oliver's kidnapping? "You don't have to help me," she whispered, the silence of the room compelling her to lower her voice. "Don't feel obligated."

"I never feel obligated," he said, lifting a hand and

smoothing her hair. "I just wish you'd been straight with me."

"I will be now."

"You'd better." He frowned and swept fallen strands of her hair behind an ear. Suddenly, his body stiffened, and he winced.

"What's wrong?"

Lowering his hand, he glided it from her knee to her thigh, his strong warm fingers settling on the hem of the nightie. "Nothing. I just got a little uncomfortable."

"Should I get up?"

"No, I don't mind."

She guessed not. Now, against her thigh, she could feel how aroused he was, and she became aware that she was sitting on his lap, on his bed, on black silk sheets, nearly naked. Sensing the direction of her thoughts, he murmured, "Sorry, Mackinley. But I can't help it when you're around."

"Who asked you to?" Stretching upward, she pressed her mouth to his. His slightly parted lips felt as warm, delicious and alive as the rest of him.

When she drew away, his hand began slowly rubbing her thigh, sending sensations spiraling through her. He whispered, "You don't owe me anything, Mackinley."

She pressed a finger to his lips. "I owe you a lot."

"I haven't done anything."

"I don't feel so alone."

He nodded. "I guess that's something."

It meant everything to her, but instead of protesting she let another silence fall. She suddenly smiled. "For a man with a gift for gab, you've gotten awfully quiet."

Male appreciation was in the eyes that fluttered between her breasts and her lips. Inhaling deeply, she savored his strong masculine scent, and then she lightly pressed his shoulders, wordlessly urging him to lie back on the bed. "Mackinley..." he said.

"Rafe..." she returned.

He went almost reluctantly, his lips still parted, in protest or anticipation—she wasn't sure which. Resting his back on the mattress, his knees curling over the edge, he caught her hand and swung it to his chest and cradled it as she threaded her fingers tightly through his. With her other hand, she traced the tattooed wreath of leaves circling his biceps. "Why green leaves?"

His eyes were seductive slits now, the lids nearly closed. He shrugged, his voice low. "Something about being young forever."

"Maybe that's not all it's cracked up to be."

"I used to think it was."

"Not now?"

He shook his head. "No."

She desperately wanted to ask the question, so she did. "Did you really want to get old with Charmaine?"

He shook his head. "No. It was just a fleeting thought."

Mackinley managed a nod, since it was exactly as she'd suspected. Rafe hadn't really been looking to settle down.

"You?" he said. "Do you miss being married?"

She sighed, trying not to notice how her panties

were making direct contact with his jeans, since her nightie was so short. "I...hung on to the illusion that things would work out," she explained, fighting her response to him. "And I still believe in marriage...know family life's what I want." But she needed to talk to Oliver, so she'd have more sense of closure. She hoped he was all right.

Rafe's voice turned hoarse. "C'mon, sweetheart. We'd better get your stuff. We'd better get you home."

She studied him a long moment. "But you don't really want me to leave yet, do you, Rafe?"

He licked dry lips. "You must be a mind reader. Because I definitely don't."

As she scooted up to straddle his hips, his hands circled her waist, feeling heavy and warm through the gown as she leaned and kissed him sweetly, almost chastely, suddenly wanting him more than she could bare, and intending to coax the man who had never needed coaxing before.

It didn't take much. After a moment, Rafe released a groan, and her lower body tightened as he rustled his hands up under her nightie and slid them into the waistband of her panties. His palms curled over her backside and his fingers gently stroked her skin. Guiding her as his hips rose, he crushed her against where he'd become so swollen.

"Let me turn off the lights," she said, her breasts suddenly hurting with the need for his mouth, her lower body feeling open and aching.

"No," he whispered. "Leave them on. I want to see you."

Embarrassed color flooded her face as a wave of longing washed over her. No man had ever made her feel this way. "I never did it with the lights on," she managed.

His smouldering eyes captured hers, the dark green irises holding disbelief. "Your ex?"

She tried to hold his gaze, but she couldn't. She glanced away. "Oliver and I had a lot of problems. It wasn't...that great, Rafe."

Fortunately, he understood it wasn't the right time for explanations, and when she looked at him again, understanding and sympathy were in his eyes.

"Don't worry," he said. "It's going to be great now."

"Really?"

"I don't make promises I can't keep."

She felt a thrill of hope, a triumphal rush of pleasure, and when Rafe flicked out his tongue, silently asking for a kiss, she leaned and caught it, kissing him back. His mouth closed down harder and his tongue delved while his hands brought her closer, his hips rolling smoothly, erotically. Feeling him so hard between her legs brought her right to the edge, and she hung there, the full building sensation making her gasp, and him shudder.

"You're such a hot woman, Mackinley Leigh," Rafe ground out, sucking a breath between gritted teeth.

"Is that so?" she whispered, feeling another rush of anticipation.

Rafe's lips were parted, his breath a soft pant, and she couldn't have been more thrilled about what she did to him. He whispered, "I'm not even sure you understand how hot yet."

"Let's find out." Gingerly, she pushed his tight T-shirt up on his flat abdomen, watching his muscles quiver. As he finished tugging off the shirt, her fingers clutched in his chest hair, her eyes following the thick dark line down to his jeans. Wanting to give him what he'd given her earlier, she leaned forward and licked his nipples, then brushed her cheeks where her mouth had been.

He groaned. "The nightgown's gorgeous," he uttered brokenly. "But let's get it off of you."

She sat up, and he bit his lower lip hard, his eyes never leaving hers. Feeling nervous in the bright light, she pulled the gown over her head, then looked down at him, fighting the urge to cover her breasts.

But Rafe very obviously liked what he saw. She blushed under his scrutiny, and yet the heat in her skin was from excitement, too.

"Are we really doing this, Mackinley?" he whispered simply, his voice heavy with awe as he urged her to lie beside him. Pushing back the bedspread, he slid with her onto black silk, his passionate gaze drifting downward, over her body. "It'll feel good to let go," he assured.

"I've been so scared."

He nodded, stroking her cheek, snuggling close. "I've lived for months with families undergoing what you've been experiencing. I'm sorry."

"I never stop thinking about it."

"You will now."

His eyes settled on hers, promising he'd sweep her away, then he tilted back her head and began torturing her with hot sharp kisses that started below an ear and turned languorously calculating by the time they reached her breasts. With every hungry stroke of his tongue, loose sobs were torn from her throat. Threading a hand in his hair, she soothed the coarse strands as he kissed her, her fingers massaging his scalp, and suddenly she arched, silently twisting, wordlessly begging him for more intimacy, but he only gorged himself on her flesh, biting and teasing, the stubble of his cheeks blessedly abrasive. His hunger fed her, and she arched again, wanting him to fill her.

Leaving a hand to tangle in his hair, her other trembled, lowering to his fly. Experimentally, she brushed her fingertips over him, frightened and excited by his size, the feathery touch sending him into excruciating agony. His eyes turned darker, almost black. Narrowed and glazed with lust, they were almost like a stranger's eyes.

"Go ahead," he urged, his voice ragged.

She knew what he meant. Hot and wet from his kisses, her breasts brushed his bare belly as she unbuckled his belt. Her heart hammering, her hands shaking, she opened the snap, then carefully lowered the zipper. Seeing how he strained a pair of tight briefs, her already unsteady breath caught. Before tonight, she'd only seen Oliver, and as she continued undressing Rafe she realized he was bigger, darker, framed by the same wild, dark untamed hair that coated his chest.

Mindlessly, she reached for him, her eyes closing in ecstasy while his mouth locked to her breast again, his tongue wild now as he reached and slid a finger under the legband of her panties. Feeling her readiness, he shivered, and she cooed something senseless, unable to believe how much he wanted her.

Scooting away, he slid off the mattress, and she watched as he reached down and fished around in the drawer of the bedside table, the muscles of his bare shoulders and back rippling. He tossed some condoms on the nightstand, ripped the foil off one with his teeth, then he turned his gaze on her again.

"Damn if you're not seriously gorgeous, Mackinley Leigh."

It was no time to be coy, but she whispered, "Really?"

His voice was a low, sexy rumble. "I wouldn't lie. And you can see what you do to me."

She most certainly could.

"Why don't you take off those panties for me, sweetheart?"

"Okay," she said breathlessly. Quickly, she stripped them down her legs, daintily whisking them over her feet, then she scooted to the edge of the bed and tossed them over, feeling jittery. Even more so as Rafe, leaning lithely, glided both his hands onto her knees, then gazed hotly down as he urged her legs apart. A second later, the touch of his mouth seared her.

"Not yet," he whispered over and over between intimate kisses that brought her where he wanted her. Only when she was teetering on the desperate edge of oblivion, her consciousness hanging by a thread, did he reach and roll on the condom.

"I'm scared," she whispered shakily, even though her whole body was on fire now and damp with perspiration. "I've only been with my husband." She wanted Rafe to know.

"*Ex*-husband," he whispered. "It's okay, Mackinley. I know what I'm doing."

She bit back a whimper. "Seems like it so far."

Before capturing her lips in a slow kiss, Rafe smiled. "This will be right. I promise." Kneeling between her legs and threading his fingers into her hair, she suddenly felt him—warm living silk—right where she was most wanting. Lifting a hand to her mouth, she gasped as he slowly pushed inside, taking his time stretching her. She slid upward with his movement, gliding on cool dark silk now, his first real thrust burning, the second making her cry with need, the third bringing relief and wild abandon. Everything inside her went dark then. Pleasure rippled through her, a sweet mindless craving...a strong sensual striving such as she'd never known she could share. Pure yearning rushed through her veins, making her heart suddenly ache. "Rafe," she whispered.

His one word sounded broken. "Yeah?"

But she was too far gone to answer, so he coiled his massive arms around her, his silken hair sweeping across her cheek, his strong forearms flexing against her sides as waves of flooding release broke over her like a waterfall, leaving her sobbing.

"Rafe," she whispered again, and as the soft whisper of the name brought his explosive climax, Mackinley held him just as tightly, feeling in that moment as if nothing in life had ever brought her this much emotion, not even her baby. Dreamily shutting her eyes, she pressed her mouth to Rafe's shoulder, and as her lips registered the feverish heat of his skin, she thought it was a damn shame he wasn't the marrying kind.

She'd craved this closeness for so long. Too long. And, yes, she thought, she could most certainly fall in love with him.

6

RAFE PAUSED beside the elevators, his footsteps stilling on the dark marble, his hands tightening around the handles of two black leather suitcases. Any anger he'd felt had vanished long ago, and now his eyes trailed from where the doorman stood under the awning outside the dimly lit lobby to Mackinley who was leaning against the unmanned front lobby desk, the database printout in a box at her feet next to her carryon.

She had captured his heart upstairs. Rafe remembered his first impressions of her—her people-pleasing perkiness, her aware brown eyes, her efforts to befriend him—and he mentally raked himself over the coals. He should have known she needed help. How had she survived? He'd coached powerful people—public figures and multinational business personnel—and yet he'd seen them fall apart while waiting for ransom calls.

But Mackinley hadn't. Instead she'd infiltrated his place and ripped off the database material. Guilt twisted inside him.

Questions about her ex plagued him, too. So far, Rafe had gotten the story in a nutshell. She'd been a new mother and still grieving her father's death when Oliver was nabbed. Since they'd been married only two years and the ink wasn't even dry on the divorce decree yet, she felt there was no proper closure to the marriage. Already, she'd paid out six million dollars in wire transfers—most of the remaining Leigh steel fortune, but then the bastards got greedy. Instead of returning Oliver, they'd bled her for the rest.

She confirmed that she'd sold off assets, including the building in which she and her mother now lived and that was previously managed by a realtor. As part of the sale agreement, she and her mother were living in the building rent free for a year. Chewing the inside of his cheek, Rafe mulled over her admission that her sex life hadn't been greatly fulfilling. Anger coiled inside him again. How could a man not want to see her satisfied? Her excited, musky scent still tortured him, as did visions of her naked, lying on black silk. He'd never forget how she'd whimpered as his hands glided down her pale thighs, or how her knees shook as his palms molded over them, urging them apart. She'd been seriously gorgeous there. Small and generously open, dusky as a seashell and glistening inside. Rafe had never been so driven to make a woman come undone. Now a damp hot shiver slid down to the small of his back.

He respected her, too. Without complaint, she'd shouldered this burden, negotiating with her ex-husband's kidnappers. While doing so, she'd even shown up for a job. Her useless ex had left her damn near a virgin as near as Rafe could tell, and yet she was determined to do whatever was necessary to save the man's sorry butt.

Even seduce me.

Rafe shifted uncomfortably. Thinking of how he'd helped Charmaine, only to be ditched, he decided he'd better fight his emotions now. Firmly, he told himself that he and Mackinley had made a deal—they'd sleep together while he helped her find Oliver. It had been her idea, right?

As he began walking again, she turned and frowned. "Suitcases?"

"I'm moving in, Mackinley."

She tucked a disheveled golden curl around an ear, then rested her thumb against her lip and bit the tip. "With me?"

He nodded. "And your mom. Until this is over." Feeling confused about his own motives, Rafe added, "I always move in with clients."

She looked uncertain. "I know, but..."

"You said they asked you to get another ten grand. Did you?"

She shook her head. "Today at lunch I sold all the remaining stocks and bonds, but I won't get the money until day after tomorrow. If they call before that..."

"I'll lend you the money," Rafe said firmly. "From now on, we're inseparable. When that phone rings, I'm going to be with you, Mackinley."

"I have to make the drop, though."

He hated putting her in danger, but knew they had no choice. He nodded curtly. "We'll catch them then. I don't want to involve too many people, but Shark will help." Rafe paused, watching the pulse in her neck flicker like a filament inside a light, quivering under transluscent, glowing skin. Setting down the suitcases, he stepped closer, brushed his knuckles against the spot, then captured her hand so she'd quit biting her thumbnail. "Are you sure the calls always come in the evening?"

"Yes. Every one." She glanced away. "What if...if he's dead?"

"He's not. They called yesterday."

Her eyes found Rafe's again. "But he's been gone so long."

"People have been returned after years," Rafe countered.

She shrugged. "I guess in the world of hostage negotiation nine months is nothing."

"Not nothing. You deserve credit for holding up the way you have."

"But what about the money I've paid?"

As he lifted his shoulders in a slight shrug, he wondered if it was his imagination, or if her eyes really held new softness now, brought by his lovemaking. "In 1975, the Born family paid sixty million for Jorge and Juan who were snatched off the street in Buenos Aires. And in '77, the Japanese government paid a bundle for thirty-eight hostages taken on a JAL DC-8."

"How did people stand the waiting?" Mackinley murmured, leaning against the lobby desk.

Rafe shook his head. "I don't know. Did you contact Citicorp, since he was working there?"

"I...told them Oliver and I were estranged. Turns out, Oliver had called, to give notice on the job."

Rafe uttered a soft curse. "No doubt the kidnappers forced him to. These guys are good, but it sounds like a small operation."

Her tawny eyebrows knitted. "Small?"

"Not a lot of people involved. They're probably using the same guys as grabbers, movers, keepers, talkers, drop men…"

"I've heard some of the terms, not all of them."

Taking a deep breath, Rafe tried not to dwell on the fact that Mackinley had been working at Ransom High Risk this whole time, holding so much stress inside. Gently he explained, "When this much money's involved, different people usually grab the victim, move him, keep him, and make the calls. But don't worry," he added, "you're a client now. I'll get him back."

"A client?" she echoed.

It was well known around the office that negotiators never slept with clients. "No," he said, changing his mind. "Not really."

"Rafe," she said. "I told you I can't pay you."

A slight smile curled his lips. "Good. Then you're definitely not a client."

"Since that's the case…" She walked into his arms, her body warm.

"You feel so good," he said huskily, his hands splaying on her lower back, gliding upward on either side of her spine, her coat feeling as soft as cashmere. Her hair was just as soft, the golden cap like corn flax. "Maybe with me in your apartment, you'll actually sleep tonight."

She didn't answer, merely gazed up at him with soft brown eyes that were alive with carnal knowledge, edgy with fear about Oliver, and shining with relief since Rafe was going to help. He liked seeing her eyes like this, with all the pretense gone.

But was there more to her wanting her ex back? Rafe sighed. He guessed he'd just have to take what was happening between them as a one-day-at-a-time proposition, then he thought of K.G. Damn if it hadn't been nice to wake up to see those trusting brown eyes, so like his mother's.

Mackinley glanced at the suitcases again. "That's a lot of clothes, Rafe. Do you think…this will take a long time?"

"One's equipment," he explained. "Bugs, tracers, a voice scrambler in case I need to place calls related to the case."

She nodded, her thumb rising to her mouth again so she could gnaw an already whittled-down nail. "Do you think the database material will help?"

Probably not, and anyway, the information was all stored in his head. "Yeah. Sure."

She looked relieved. "Mom's going to be glad you're helping us."

"What about you, Mackinley?"

"Me, too."

He knew that, but he wanted to hear her say it. Stretching her arms around his neck, she hugged him, and he leaned down and kissed her fully, feeling warmth drizzle through him. The kiss was special. *She* was special.

Moving back a fraction, he forced himself to ask what was uppermost on his mind. "Are there other reasons why you're trying so hard to get Oliver back? Or are you doing it just because he's K.G.'s dad?" Rafe felt like a fool for asking, but she'd said her marriage still needed closure. With so much money at stake, people often ran straight to the cops, but people desperately in love wouldn't take that risk. Mackinley's eyes darted away from his, and he hoped she wasn't going to be evasive.

"Like I said, Oliver and I..."

Had problems? Rafe didn't trust himself to finish the sentence for her. Her ex was Rafe's polar opposite—light complexioned and slight of build, with blond hair and intelligent eyes framed by wire-rim glasses. While Rafe didn't want to make comparisons, he couldn't stand the thought of Oliver making love with Mackinley.

"He...lost interest when I got pregnant," she continued. "I guess some men do. He was in South America on business when the baby was born, and that's when..."

"He was snatched."

"I guess..." She shrugged, her eyes searching Rafe's for understanding. "My parents had such a perfect marriage. I mean, they were always laughing and going places together. When I was a kid, I felt like a third wheel, but it never really bothered me."

Rafe had no idea where she was heading with this, but he said, "I felt the same way, but for different reasons. Dad and the guys were always playing cards, shooting pool...I always felt like a tagalong, especially back when he was still in the army."

"Your dad loves you."

He nodded. "We had fun. Still do."

"I loved watching my folks together." She paused, shaking her head ruefully. "I guess I've been hoping that when Oliver's released, he'll see the baby and..."

Fall in love with you again? Rafe steeled himself against the thought. Besides, from what Rafe had been told, it wasn't even remotely realistic. They were divorced. His hands tightened involuntarily on her back and he drew her closer, offering a physical reminder of what had happened upstairs. His voice turned gruff. "You said Oliver didn't give you what you needed."

"No. He didn't, and he didn't really want the baby. He was overwhelmed by all the new responsibilities, I think."

Rafe's jaw set. Who wouldn't want K.G.? "I can't believe that."

Her eyes softened. "You like him, don't you?"

He nodded. During their trip to Chinatown yesterday, everybody had assumed Rafe was K.G.'s dad, and he'd enjoyed playing the role. He liked...being a family man. After all, he'd never had a normal family. "What guy wouldn't want that?"

"Oliver said he wanted a family, but I think he got scared about the level of commitment. Or maybe... some men don't like kids."

"They're crazy."

She tilted her head. "Do you like kids?"

"Sure," Rafe returned easily. "Since I met K.G."

She nodded. "I thought Oliver and I were going to be so happy, just like my parents. I thought he'd be as loving as my dad..." Her voice suddenly broke. "Oh, Rafe, I miss my dad."

Rafe could imagine. As much of a pain in the butt as Jack Ransom had been since the synergy workshop, he and Rafe were as tight as canned sardines. "I know what you mean. Maybe because I didn't have two parents, Jack's always been the world to me."

An almost wistful smile tugged the corners of her

mouth. "I can tell. You fight, but you love each other so much."

"Yeah."

Her eyes drifted, looking thoughtful, and Rafe continued staring into them, watching how the red and gold flecks caught in the dim light. Suddenly, they focused again, sharp on his. "I can't let my son grow up without a dad, Rafe."

"He won't." Rafe wasn't sure why he promised that. It was premature, he knew, but even he could admit that he'd fantasized that the right man to father K.G. was him.

She eyed him a long moment. "Is it true victims come to care for their kidnappers?" she suddenly said.

He squinted at her. "Yeah. It's called the Stockholm Syndrome."

She frowned. "Why?"

"In 1973, four Swedes were held in a Stockholm bank vault for six days during a heist. They grew to rely on the robbers."

Another small smile curled Mackinley's mouth. "So, I could fall for my captor?"

Despite the circumstances, he found himself smiling back. "I haven't captured you."

"But you could Rafe," Mackinley whispered, her husky voice suddenly fervent. Suddenly, she rose to her toes and brushed her mouth across his. "If you tried, Rafe, I think you most certainly could."

PRESSING HER CHEEK to the pillow and staring into the pitch darkness, Mackinley let her mind wander from thoughts of Rafe, to her parents' perfect marriage, then to her son. "K.G.," she whispered, liking the name, unable to see the crib in the dark, but knowing he was asleep. Suddenly, she realized the pillow smelled of Rafe, and she sighed, inhaling deeply, pulling the scent into her lungs.

She wished he was sleeping with her instead of on the living room couch, but even though she was divorced, she feared her mother would be scandalized. Just as Mackinley suspected, her mom was as relieved as she that Rafe was helping them, and Rafe had spent the hour before bedtime questioning Barbara.

Bedtime. Mackinley swallowed hard, recalling how he'd stood before her earlier, naked and aroused, his body coated with dark tangled hair. Too bad she believed in marriage, she thought. Making love with Rafe was enough to make any woman consider a lifetime of no-strings-attached sex. However, her parents had provided her with a strong example of marital bliss, and Rafe Ransom, unfortunately, wasn't the marrying kind. Tonight, he'd come right out and admitted he hadn't really wanted to settle down with Charmaine after all.

Mackinley's heart squeezed, pulling inside her chest. She'd been such a damn fool to assume life would naturally bring her a perfect, loving relationship. She'd met Oliver in college, and she'd pressured him to marry—she could admit that now—but only because she'd thought they'd become closer, like her parents.

Instead she'd gotten two years of bittersweet memories. During her pregnancy, at a time when their intimacy should have been deepening, Oliver had begun finding fault and his criticisms had broken her heart.

Which was why she was so determined to talk to him. She needed to understand the nature of their mistakes, so she could move on. And yes, she'd held on to the fantasy that he'd see their son and fall in love with her again. Divorced couples reunited all the time, she'd thought. Why couldn't she work things out with Oliver?

Because of Rafe Ransom.

After tonight, things could never be the same. While she knew Rafe wasn't looking for marriage, the intimacy of his lovemaking convinced her that she couldn't settle again for less. And yet she was concerned for Oliver's safe return. Every time she looked at the Polaroid photographs, Mackinley's heart lurched. Oliver was unwashed, and his clothes looked so ragged....

He'd been such an impeccable dresser. Swallowing hard, she suddenly remembered a gown she'd bought when she was pregnant. It was of white silk and she'd been sure Oliver would love it. Just weeks before the baby came, she'd put it on and patiently waited for him to join her in bed. But right before he switched off the lights, she'd seen disgust in his eyes. He couldn't even hide it. It was as if she couldn't be both a mother and an object of desire. Even now, her skin flamed from the rejection which she'd tried so hard to deny. Why couldn't Oliver accept their family? He was supposed to share in the joy of the baby....

Maybe he would have eventually. But then Oliver had been brutally taken from them.

Rafe would find him, though. And surely, when Oliver saw K.G., he'd at least want to be a father. Every boy needed a man in his life.

Suddenly, the door cracked opened. A sliver of light shone through before Rafe's huge shadowy body filled it. He was bare-chested and barefoot, wearing low-slung white sweat pants.

She kept her voice low. "Rafe?"

"Yeah," he whispered, slipping into the room. As he soundlessly shut the door, his shadowy body was swallowed by the darkness. Silent as night, he came to her bed, pulled back the covers and wordlessly tried to lie down beside her. Finding that there wasn't enough room, he pulled her on top of him, and her legs trailed between his as her hands clasped behind his neck. Her bare feet slid over his. "You have really big feet, Rafe," she whispered.

"You should have seen them when I was a puppy," he whispered back.

The comment so completely jarred her from her darker thoughts that her shoulders shook with silent mirth. Despite what was happening with Oliver, Rafe was bringing her hope. "What are you doing in here?"

His voice was throaty. "Checking on you."

She snuggled against him. "I couldn't sleep. I was thinking."

Huge hands slid around her, their warmth seeping through her nightshirt as they pressed the small of her back. "Thinking's not good, Mackinley. Women should never do that."

She kicked him lightly. "But I couldn't sleep."

He planted a gentle kiss on the top of her head. "You will now," he whispered.

And she did.

7

RAFE BECAME HER fantasy lover.

All week, after her mother fell asleep, he'd been visiting Mackinley's bed like some storybook dream man. In the dark, he loved her every way possible. Sometimes it was sweet and gentle. Other times, he'd grope her like a teenager, his movements hot and frenzied until she was biting back sobs of need, her breaths harsh and shaky.

By day, she couldn't keep her eyes off him. He was insisting she rehash every conversation she'd had with the kidnappers, but the phone still hadn't rung, and nothing could be done until the kidnappers demanded the ten thousand dollars, which was now in her hot little hands. Just moments ago, she'd been busy, checking up on the photographs, which Rafe had sent to a lab, and then Jack had called everyone to the conference room, to hear the presentations she and Rafe were to give.

"Being a single parent's definitely not easy," Rafe was saying as he paced by the conference room table with K.G. slung around his hip. The baby had become so comfortable there that Mackinley's mom said Rafe might as well have been born a marsupial. He said, "Babies require more than I ever would have guessed."

"Absolutely!" said Jack excitedly. "No woman should raise a baby alone. I was sure you'd come to this conclusion, son."

Rafe tried, and failed to achieve, his usual acerbic tone. "Dad, if you already knew everything, why did Mackinley and I need to go through with this impossible exercise?"

"I didn't know *everything*." Jack glanced significantly between Mackinley and Rafe. "Just *some* things. And it seems to me that it's always best for a child to have two parents."

Jack obviously had the two particular parents in mind.

Silencer put his elbows on the table, his suit sleeves sliding down toward his elbows. He glanced around the crowded table. "Did you get him to change diapers Mackinley?"

Mackinley raised an eyebrow innocently. "Rafe or K.G.?"

Everyone laughed.

She'd already offered her words of wisdom on the trials and tribulations of being a boss, and now, as Rafe continued with his report, she took in the men around the table. If anybody at Ransom High Risk thought it was unusual to bring a baby to work, they hadn't ventured a word of criticism. Rafe assured her he only wanted to bring K.G. in order to save money on day care, since her mom had started a promising job in the administrative offices at the Museum of History, but Mackinley noticed Rafe was doting on the baby. So were the assistants from the Francesca agency; most were career focused, but they were taking advantage of the opportunity to ask questions about motherhood.

"Babies often cry in the night," Rafe was saying with a sigh. "And then there are the midnight feedings." Rafe shot Mackinley a quick, devilish smile. "It's amazing how hungry you can get in the wee hours."

"It is," Mackinley agreed solemnly.

Shark offered a knowing chuckle. "I'll bet."

Apparently whatever vibrations were passing between her and Rafe were hardly going unnoticed, and the men at Ransom High Risk were warming to her. "It was such a wonderful exercise," she teased now, matching Shark's knowing tone, "that maybe Shark might benefit from it next."

"That's the wonderful thing about synergy," Shark quickly returned. "One couple can produce a win-win for everybody."

The entire group rapidly murmured thanks.

"Really," emphasized Silencer. "I've learned so much."

"Babies are swell," assured Magnum.

Jack Ransom couldn't have looked more pleased. "We can thank my friend at the sugar refinery! Would you two say this exercise has been a win-win?"

Mackinley suddenly sighed, thinking of the long loving nights she and Rafe had shared. Maybe the pleasure was fleeting, but Rafe's lovemaking held an undeniable healing power that was allowing her to finally process the emotions of her marriage. "Yes, I most certainly do."

Rafe looked equally satisfied. "Nothing," he assured, "beats synergy."

MACKINLEY GASPED, and Rafe's heart pounded as she snatched up the phone. "It's them?" he whispered, his eyes instinctively scanning her apartment. "The kidnappers?"

She waited expectantly, then shook her head, dropping the phone beside her on the couch. She was sitting cross-legged, and now she snuggled against Rafe, pressing a hand to her heart as if to still its rapid beat. Raising her voice, she called, "No cause for alarm, Mom. It was a wrong number." Her voice lowered. "Wrong number," she repeated. "Can you believe that?"

He frowned. "On the cell phone?"

She nodded, her eyes tracing the line that connected the phone to a self-activating tape recorder that now turned itself off. "Rafe, I feel like they'll never call. It's been a week. Do you think something's happened?"

"No, they'll call. Meantime, have some more popcorn."

"Thanks but no thanks. Are you always this calm?"

"Only when gorgeous women are relying on me. Now try to watch the movie," he whispered. Mackinley continued to look worried even after her eyes returned to the TV. Romantic comedies were her favorites, big splashy Hollywood pictures with happy endings, and surprisingly, Rafe found he didn't mind watching them with her.

He lifted one of her hands, then he laid it on his palm, and brushed a thumb gently across two bitten-down fingertips she'd wrapped with bandages. Since the first night they were together, he'd come to see the bitten nails as symbolic of the anxiety she'd suffered alone. Now he sighed. Damn if something wasn't happening to his emotions over which he had no control. He glanced toward the other room, where her mother was now reading again, then at Mackinley.

Sensing his attention, she said, "Something on your mind?"

Yeah. You. Us. Your ex-husband. Rafe was itching to negotiate his release, but the more involved he became with Mackinley, the more he feared her issues with her ex weren't resolved. She referred to him as her husband, rather than her ex, and she was sure, once he was found—if he was found—that he'd have a change of heart regarding fatherhood.

"Rafe?" Mackinley prompted.

He shrugged. "Just thinking." He draped an arm around her, curling a palm over her shoulder. "I like how you look right now."

"Now? In my flannel nightgown?"

"I meant your eyes don't look so tired anymore."

Tilting her head, she sent him a sideways glance, her brown eyes sparkling with awareness, her lips twitching mischievously. "With you here, I'm sleeping better."

"I put a smile on your face?"

Lifting a hand, she absently finger-combed her artful cap of waves, and when a lock fell onto her forehead, he brushed it away. She said, "You most certainly do."

But was that all it meant for her? he wondered as her eyes returned to the TV. And shouldn't it be enough for him? Leaning back a fraction, he looked through the window. Outside, the temperature had risen and the expected snow had turned to rain. Taxis were bumper to bumper and red flashes from taillights shone on the wet pavement. "No snow," he murmured.

She shook her head. "Only in the burbs."

He withdrew his gaze from the crowded streets. "Ever think about living there?"

She squinted. "You mean in New Jersey? Or Connecticut?"

"Yeah."

"Maybe." She gazed at him thoughtfully. "I don't know. I grew up in the city, and Oliver and I lived here because it was so convenient. He was uptown, at Citicorp, and I was working as a translator at the Constellation Publishing Group."

"So you figured you'd stay in the city?"

"Yes," she said. "But that was before K.G. If I had a choice, I guess I'd like to work part-time and move somewhere else, so K.G. would have more room to play. A real yard. Friends."

Rafe narrowed his eyes. "Hmm. And why didn't you change your name when you got married?"

She squinted at him. "You're full of questions."

"Just wondering."

As she shook her head, the sudden sadness Rafe saw in her eyes touched him. "My dad was sick when I got married. I...just couldn't give up his name, Rafe." She thought another minute, then continued, "Anyway, someday I'd like to try living somewhere new. You?"

"I've been in the city a long time. But maybe." He wondered what the burbs would be like. Somehow, as he'd begun to share life with Mackinley, her mother and K.G., his mind kept returning to the idea. He'd often lived with families during hostage negotiations, so he was accustomed to slipping into other people's lives and adjusting to their rhythms. But this wasn't a regular case. And now, for the first time, Rafe was worried. When this was over, he'd miss how Barbara mothered him, and the casual banter and talk of the baby's progress he shared with Mackinley while they cleared the table or did the dishes.

The only thing Rafe wouldn't miss was the tension of waiting for the phone to ring. He stared a long hard moment at the cell phone. Who was holding Oliver Spain? And why weren't they calling? His lips compressing grimly, Rafe tried not to think the worst. Better, he thought, to keep focused on more positive topics. "Ever think of having other kids?"

Her voice was low, barely audible. "I...well..." She sighed. "Oh, Rafe, I can't even think about that. We don't even know what's happened to Oliver. He's never even seen his son."

But I want you to think about the future. Feeling vaguely disgruntled, Rafe turned his mind to the case. "Sorry," he murmured gruffly, drawing her closer against his side. "I shouldn't have asked."

"It's okay." She rubbed her head against his chest. "The thing is, I do want other kids. But...I just feel as if this will never be over."

"It will," Rafe promised, dropping a kiss on the top of her head.

"You sound convinced. How do you know?"

Because it's always over—eventually. And because your family can't go on like this much longer. Rafe just wished, like a Hollywood movie, it would have a happy ending. Unfortunately, kidnappers didn't play by Hollywood's rules. "Because I want it to be," Rafe finally said. He wanted to know exactly where Mackinley stood with her ex...and whether there was a chance of him, Rafe, having a future with her.

And right now, the only way to find out the truth was to negotiate Spain's release.

WRAPPING AN ARM tightly around K.G., Mackinley bounced him on her hip and glanced toward the living room, where Rafe was watching televised sports. "You okay, Mom?"

"Fine, dear," Barbara said as she smoothed a palm over the cover of a book she'd been reading at the dining table. She stared at Mackinley a long moment, then smiled ruefully. "You know," she suddenly said, "I've always tried to protect you, dear, but maybe I was wrong."

Mackinley pulled out a chair and seated herself. "What?"

Leaning toward her daughter, Barbara smoothed a hand over Mackinley's hair, then her eyes dropped to the baby. "The older he gets," Barbara continued, "the more you'll understand the desire to sugarcoat things for him."

Mackinley squinted, wondering what her mother was driving at. "Meaning?"

"Mackinley." Barbara's pragmatic tone held more censure than Mackinley had ever heard in it. "What I wanted to say was that your father was a good man. I loved him..."

Mackinley's lips parted in astonishment. "Of course you loved him!"

Taking a deep breath, Barbara continued, "But he was flawed and life with him wasn't always easy."

Mackinley's heart hammered. "But you had the perfect marriage," she protested. "You were always together, always laughing...so in love."

"You saw what we wanted you to see."

"Are you saying you didn't love Daddy?"

Barbara shook her head vigorously. "Of course not. But when I was your age I had so many ambitions. I've been thinking about that now, since I'm working again. When I was with your father, I never worked. He needed me to play the corporate wife."

Mackinley felt as if she'd been living in a world of illusions. "But you were happy...?"

Her mother's hand closed over hers and squeezed. "Always. Just not in the way I expected. You made me happy, and this baby's going to make you happy, too. But life's never what you expect, Mackinley, so you've got to grab happiness, even in circumstances like ours." Barbara quickly rushed on. "I know you and Rafe are sleeping together."

Mackinley gulped. "Sorry...we've tried to be quiet."

Sighing, Barbara bent closer again, her eyes warm with love. "Dear, it's not that. I'm just afraid your idealization of my marriage is going to make you feel loyal to Oliver. And it shouldn't. Not if you're falling in love with another man."

Mackinley was stunned. "Oliver's been *kidnapped*, mother."

Sadness clouded Barbara's eyes. "And Rafe's searching for him. But I can plainly see you're falling in love." She squeezed her daughter's hand again. "I'm warning you, dear," she said softly. "You're divorced now. Don't go with the rulebook. Go with your heart."

8

JUST OUR LUCK, Rafe thought three days later when the call came. *We would be in the Humvee.* He and Mackinley had just dropped K.G. with Barbara and were headed to Balducci's to pick up a chocolate mousse pie for dessert, Rafe's treat, when the ringing sounded. Staring down at the automatically activating tape recorder between the seats, Rafe was reminded of his and Mackinley's real situation. They were spending cozy domestic evenings together, yes, but only because of a man named Oliver Spain.

"Yes?" Mackinley said, depressing the phone's On button as Rafe gripped the wheel, zigzagging between two taxis and swerving to the curb in front of a Japanese dojo. "Sorry, I can't hear you," she continued loudly, staring through the tinted windshield at dark sidewalks that were thick with rush-hour crowds. "You'll have to speak up. I'm driving in heavy traffic." There was a pause. "So, you want me to take the ten thousand dollars to the West Fourth Street subway station, is that right? You'll meet me in ten minutes?" She glanced at Rafe's watch, her hand curling so tightly around the receiver that her knuckles turned white. "I can't bring the money in a brown bag," she protested as Rafe reached silently beneath the seat, pulled up the duffel and rested it in his lap, then nosed into the stream of traffic again, heading for the station. "I'm in the car," she continued. "I don't have access to another bag...right now, the money's in a paisley bag...yes, yes, it's all here. You said ten thousand, so I got ten thousand. But I want my husband back."

The party on the other end talked, then Mackinley said, "Ten minutes is too soon. What if I can't make it? Okay, you want me to put the bag on top of the blue trash can. You're sure it's the only blue can on the platform?" She repeated the directions. "Okay. I'll keep my hand on top of the bag, but turn my eyes away from the track."

They were near the station, but she was buying time; Rafe's quick glance of approval was followed by a rush of concern, since her eyes suddenly widened in alarm. "No, I swear I'm alone," she insisted. "Most certainly alone...no, I didn't call the police. I gave you my word." She ran a free hand nervously through her hair, ruffling the already windblown waves; obviously, she was fighting panic. "You have to believe me. I've told no one. Stop it—" She stared worriedly at Rafe. "Please, stop saying you'll kill him. You'll get your money in ten minutes. Just don't hurt Oliver. I'm begging you. What do you mean you're watching me? If you're watching me, then you know I'm alone. Look, we've got to nego—"

The phone went dead. Swiftly depressing the Off button, Mackinley dropped the receiver into her lap and spoke rapid-fire, her eyes riveted on the windshield. "West Fourth Street," she said as Rafe turned the corner onto West Thirteenth.

"I'm circling around," he said, "so we can park on Bleeker. Did he say where to meet him in the station?"

"The D train track."

Rafe punched the gas. "And you know the station?"

"Like the back of my hand."

She would. It was her old neighborhood. "It's a two-tier station, right? From what I remember, the A trains are on the ground level."

"He told me to go in, head straight downstairs. The D trains are another level down."

"You have tokens?"

"Tokens," she echoed, pressing a hand anxiously to her mouth as she wrenched her gaze from the windshield, opened her handbag and clawed in her wallet. "If I have to stop and buy tokens, I'll never make it in time," she murmured. "I usually have some. But I don't know Rafe. I don't think you should come with me."

Was she crazy? "Here's the plan," he countered. "You go first. I'll follow at a distance, and once we're in the station I'll stay a few feet behind. Apparently, this guy intends to approach you directly. Even if he talks to you, don't turn around. Things might get ugly if you accidentally see what he looks like." Rafe tried not to consider that this might be a last rendezvous, and the man was going to... An image of Mackinley being pushed onto the tracks made every muscle in Rafe's body tense.

"But Rafe, the man said he'd kill Oliver." Finding tokens, she paused a second, then dropped one into Rafe's coat pocket, shuddering. "This time, he sounded serious. Really, I don't think we should risk it. Why don't you wait outside for me?"

Rafe considered the options. It was already dark, everyone was rushing home from work and the

Greenwich Village streets were pure madness. Stopping for a light, Rafe watched a pink-haired teenager on a skateboard fly between two vampirish goths in long dark coats who looked as if they'd just stepped from an Anne Rice novel. "Was it the same man?"

"I don't know. His voice sounded garbled."

"Probably scrambled."

She reached to grip the dashboard as the light changed. "He said if he thought I'd double-crossed him, he'd kill Oliver." Her voice caught. "He sounded...desperate."

"Death threats are always good," Rafe assured her. "Did he say exactly *how* he intended to kill?"

"No. Just that he would if I called the cops."

"Good," Rafe repeated. "The more dangerous the nabbers, the more specific they like to get." Most liked to talk torture. K&R wasn't a pretty business. Everything was topsy-turvy. Sometimes, especially south of the border, the cops *were* the bad guys. Everyone was a suspect. Glancing at Mackinley, Rafe suddenly wanted out. He took in her angelic cap of golden waves which looked brown in the Humvee's dark interior, her upturned nose and delicate lips. Hell, he thought. If Jack retired, maybe Rafe could manage the office and move to the Jersey suburbs.

"Rafe?"

He blinked. It was definitely the wrong time to be thinking about mortgages and picket fences. "Yeah?" He swerved a quick left onto Seventh, then took another left onto Bleeker.

"I don't want you coming," Mackinley repeated decisively, pulling on her gloves and lifting the paisley bag from his lap as he backed into a parallel parking space.

"What?" he barked. "Are you serious?"

"If he sees someone's helping me, he'll kill Oliver."

"Sweetheart," Rafe countered, turning off the engine and scanning the sidewalk for suspicious faces, "if he's making threats, Oliver's probably still alive." But maybe not for long, Rafe added silently. Her ex had been somebody's cash cow, but now that Mackinley was approaching a zero bank balance, he could quickly turn into a liability. Not that Rafe intended to share that information with her.

"But you didn't hear the voice," she protested, gripping the paisley bag by a worn leather handle.

"I will later on the tape." Unless horns, motors and sirens had destroyed the sound quality. "And don't worry. He won't see me. I've been doing this for years. Just keep low when you get out. Circle around the front of the hummer, then straighten up and head for the station. Stay alert, but look casual. Whatever you do, don't look back at me. I'll be right behind you."

"Not this time."

"Mackinley," he said, fighting exasperation, "as soon as the guy comes for the bag, I'm going to grab him."

"But I'm telling you, Rafe, there was something wrong with the voice...something scary." She shuddered again.

"We've waited a week for this call. We can't blow it."

"Dammit," she muttered. "Have it your way."

She was angry, but she'd come around. "I'm right

behind you," he repeated. "Which side of the track do we meet him on? Up or downtown?"

Mackinley glared at him a long moment. "Downtown."

"Good. Be careful."

Still looking fuming mad, she abruptly swung open the door and dropped to the street, gripping the bag. Rafe's heart missed a beat as the door slammed, and he tried to tell himself that her anger was only misplaced nervousness. Damn if he wanted to send her traipsing down Sixth Avenue with ten large, though. People in this neighborhood had definitely been annihilated for less.

Through the tinted glass, he watched her move between a businessman and a manor-born blonde who was walking two Doberman's with black leather spiked collars. So far, no one seemed to be watching Mackinley. Since it was still rush hour, her camel coat and classy pumps didn't even make her stand out. "Amazing," he muttered. Even though she was carrying ten thousand bucks in her hand, she moved up the avenue as naturally as breathing. Waiting as long as he could stand, which meant exactly two more seconds, Rafe hopped out of the Humvee and followed at a distance.

Up ahead, she passed a news kiosk and a pizza joint, then vanished down the dusty station steps. Rafe fought the urge to run after her. What if the directions were a ruse? What if the guy was going to snatch the cash now?

By the time Rafe's hips slammed through the turnstile, Mackinley was gone again. He glanced around. Still no one suspicious. Just as he headed down a tunnel toward the lower tracks, a swarm of just-released passengers elbowed toward him from the opposite direction. Gritting his teeth, he pushed back. He had to get downstairs. He glared at his watch, then past some movie posters pasted to the walls. There were only a few minutes left. And there'd been no time to prepare for the drop. How was the man going to approach her? Would he hurt her?

And where was she? Rafe walked the length of the downtown platform, barely noticing the stuffy dank air and how the tile walls lent the old station an aquatic air, as if it were an emptied-out swimming pool. She said the downtown track, didn't she?

His eyes darted toward the stairs leading to the A trains, then he looked across the tracks. From far down the tunnel, an uptown D train was approaching now, just a streak of silver. And then he saw Mackinley.

"Damn," he cursed. She'd lied. She was on the uptown platform. Separated from him by the rails, she'd placed the paisley bag on a blue trash can. She'd been afraid the man wouldn't be captured and that he'd see Rafe and kill Oliver.

Their eyes met, just as Rafe realized the kidnapper was probably on the approaching train. No doubt he was going to leap off, snag the bag and escape upstairs, fading into the crowds. Rafe considered leaping on the tracks to get to Mackinley, but the train would hit him, so he bolted for the stairs, knowing he'd never make it. As he ran down the tunnel and passed the turnstiles, he heard metal screech as the train's unoiled wheels braked on the tracks. On the other side of the station, he imagined the train doors opening. The kidnapper was stepping onto the platform, heading for Mackinley...

Rafe ran downstairs, onto the uptown platform—and right into her. She gasped. His hands closed around her upper arms just as the train began pulling out again. She was as breathless as he, but probably from fear. He said, "Where is he?"

"Gone. He grabbed the bag. Got back on the train."

"Did you see him?"

"No. I did what he said. I kept my hand on the bag and looked away, but I felt him grab it."

Rafe stared down, fear for her safety getting the best of him. "I thought you wanted my help," he growled.

The worst thing was, she didn't look the least bit penitent. "I told you. He sounded serious this time. If he saw you, he might have killed Oliver. And I couldn't live with myself. So, we'll just have to come up with another plan. There simply wasn't time to argue with you in the car. We'll have to try to locate him through phone records or the tapes."

"What do you think I'm trying to do?" Knowing his eyes were shooting daggers, Rafe reminded himself that he did trust her perception. Maybe her deception had protected Oliver. Rafe loosened his grip on her upper arm, but he still couldn't contain his anger. "Mind telling me what's going on here Mackinley?"

She glared up at him. "I told you," she seethed. "I'm keeping Oliver alive. And you'd be more help if you quit seeing him as your personal adversary."

The lie rolled off his tongue. "I don't."

She shot him a furious look. "Oh, really?"

"Okay. Maybe I do. But maybe I should."

"You think I'm somehow using you, Rafe?" She

stared at him, looking offended. "You think I'm not interested in what's going on between us? That I'm going back to Oliver?"

Rafe was vaguely aware that people were starting to stare. "Are you?"

"I don't know," she snapped. "And why does it matter? What are you looking for Rafe? A relationship?"

Relationship. It was the first time either of them had mentioned that word. "Don't we have one?"

"For now."

That got his back up. "Sweetheart," he couldn't help but say, "when the sun goes down and I'm in your bed, you don't seem to be complaining."

"Please, Rafe. You're hardly the committal type."

As if she'd know. His jaw set. "Seems to me I've committed to helping you out of this jam." And for all his trouble, she was going to walk. Just like Charmaine.

Her lower lip trembled with what looked like barely suppressed fury, and now her brown eyes were flashing. "You seem not to have noticed the ordeal I've just been through. But since you're so committed, why don't you look for some clues or something, Rafe." She brushed past him. "I believe I need some fresh air."

Staring at her retreating back, he didn't know which he wanted to do—kiss or kill. So he did neither. He simply watched her head regally upstairs, deciding to cool off before he followed. "So much for teamwork," he muttered, thinking it was time he struck out with his own investigation.

Already, Rafe knew Oliver had lost investment capital while working for Citicorp. Maybe some ruined investors had kidnapped Oliver for revenge, to get their money back. That explained why the calls were so polite. Compared to the usual fare, Mackinley was getting cocktail party conversation. Guys who went for big wads like hers usually thrived on fear. As an opening gambit, they'd call to say they were dismembering a person, then they'd slam down the phone. Period. No questions. And maybe, just maybe, they'd call back.

Rafe knew how to handle guys such as that. But when it came to negotiations, it was Mackinley who was giving him trouble. Sure, Rafe would like to think she'd been fishing for admissions of his feelings just now—except, in reality, she'd lied to protect Spain. Which meant she'd try to go back to Spain, if the man was ever released.

And that left Rafe between a rock and a hard place since the last thing he wanted to do was negotiate for the freedom of his rival.

"It's just as you suspected, Rafe." Shark put up his legs, unapologetically crossing his feet on the conference room table and exposing burnt-orange ankle socks that matched his suit and the laces of wing tips.

Rafe stared. "You know," he said, "I seriously hope you're wearing these tacky suits in silent protest because of Mackinley's and Dad's new dress code."

Shark chuckled. "You know me well, my friend. A woman who worked in costuming on *Guys and Dolls* on Broadway loaned me the suits. I figured if Mackinley and your old man saw enough of them, they'd let us wear jeans to work again. The scheme's not

working, but at least you've solved Mackinley's case."
Shark gave Rafe a thumbs-up sign and sighed contentedly. "Ah," Shark added, "another day, another two thousand dollars. Excellent."

It wasn't. Four days ago, Rafe and Mackinley had driven away from the train station in a weighty, seething silence that hadn't broken until the next afternoon when they'd finally shared a bowl of ice cream. Now things were finally on an even keel again, and Rafe wanted to keep it that way.

And now this. He hated what he'd just discovered and wished he wasn't so powerless to stop it. "She's broke," he said aloud as he stared murderously down at the tape recorder and an open file folder containing an inch-high stack of evidence, including a picture of Oliver Spain outside the house where he'd been staying. "So, she's not paying me." And Rafe didn't care. He just wished Spain hadn't been placing the ransom calls to Mackinley using a voice scrambler. Nine months ago, Spain had simultaneously lost millions at his job and decided fatherhood wasn't for him, so he'd masterminded his own disappearance. Using everything he'd learned about the Leigh estate during his marriage, he'd financially drained Mackinley.

Now gazing through the interior window at Mackinley who was bouncing K.G. on her hip while talking to Jack, Rafe had to fight to suppress his fury over the injustice. She looked so sweet and innocent, wearing a crisp white blouse tucked into the tan wool skirt that swept opaque brown tights. "Maybe we should lock up Spain before I tell her," Rafe finally said.

Shark had been staring down, absently fingering a wide, wildly patterned royal blue and mustard yellow tie. Now he glanced up, his gaze far sharper than his outfit. "Really? You think she'll go after Spain physically or something, when she finds out he ripped her off?"

Rafe ran a hand raggedly through his hair. "It's not her style, but she'll react. When it comes to betrayal, you never know." He just wondered if *he* was about to be betrayed.

"Right." Shark sighed. "Remember that lady in Dallas?"

The woman's husband had been kidnapped while on his way to visit his mistress. The wife, who'd been lounging on the deck of the swimming pool when Rafe and Shark delivered the news, had casually removed the towel covering her bathing suit and calmly walked to the driveway while rolling the towel. After inserting it into the gas tank of her husband's brand new Mercedes-Benz, she'd lit the towel with a disposable lighter, hopped into her own convertible and sped away, shouting, "Tell him I hope he gets everything he deserves. Let his lousy girlfriend pay his ransom!"

Shark, who'd extricated the towel and saved the Mercedes before it exploded, now murmured philosophically, "Mackinley will either go ballistic or not even believe you. You know that's usually the case. For some reason, women still trust their ex-husbands. It's your call, Rafe."

Rafe growled, "Wish we'd found him sooner." *Like nine months sooner*.

"If wishes were horses, beggars would ride."

"Keep it up, Shark," Rafe snapped, "and Columbia'll offer you an honorary doctorate in philosophy."

Shark looked touched. "You mean that, Rafe?"

Rafe didn't bother to respond. He stared down at the pictures of Spain, holding up a Spanish-language newspaper. As it turned out, the Polaroid film had been purchased at a Long Island convenience store, and some fingerprints Rafe had lifted from Spain's belongings matched a smudge on a corner of one of the snapshots.

"Well, anyway," Shark reminded him, "time takes time."

Unfortunately, while time was taking its good old time, McKinley had been living in fear, worrying about a man who didn't deserve her concern. "Maybe I'll kill him," Rafe said, thinking it was tempting. "And tell her we never found him."

"She's probably never going to get her money back."

Rafe nodded. If he'd only known sooner, Rafe could have saved her fortune. Staring at her, he felt his chest constrict. She was so smart, but gullible, and damn if Rafe wasn't...well, in something with her.

"Any ideas about where Spain put it?" asked Shark.

Rafe shook his head. "He's been lying low, playing it smart. The money's probably spread around American banks, deposited under false names. Spain was a banker so he knows how banks work." But then, so did Rafe. And one way or another, he'd get Mackinley's money back.

Shark stared toward the cubicles. "Where'd she go?"

Rafe glanced through the window again. "She's probably getting ready to head home. I'll tell her and her mom as soon as we get to her place." Rafe's gaze suddenly sharpened, his anger surfacing again. "I guess the whole western world knows where Spain is now?"

Shark shrugged. "Once we knew he wasn't in danger, I started calling everybody I know."

"On both sides of the law?"

"Sure, why not? Spain paid some guys to overnight him the newspapers. Anyway, I didn't think talking to our people in the Latin quarter would hurt. We just needed Spain's location, which we got." Shark paused. "You know, if you want to wait to tell Mackinley, you can. Spain hasn't moved for months. He's not going anywhere."

Rafe wouldn't rest easy until Spain was behind bars. "True. I wish fewer people knew his location, though."

"He's not dangerous. Just a con man."

"Yeah, that's how it looks." Rafe paced the room, then leaned against the exterior window. He stared down at a graffiti covered newsstand and a Chinese laundry. Suddenly, he felt tired. He'd lived in the city too long, and when he wasn't here he was holed up with clients, often in South America, in humorless walled compounds protected by video surveillance and vicious dogs. "You ever think of moving to the burbs?" He asked, turning from the window.

"And miss all this action? Are you kidding?" Shark looked stunned, then comprehension dawned. "Don't tell me you're considering getting a place with Mackinley? One with an AstroTurf yard, some cats and dogs, rug rats crawling everywhere?"

That's exactly what Rafe was thinking. "Who knows?"

"Well first, lock up husband *numero uno.*" Shark chuckled softly. "Even with Charmaine, it was clear you were starting to get the settle-down bug." He grinned. "I just hope that bug's not catching."

Rafe ignored him. He was going to hate telling Mackinley and her mother the truth about Spain. He'd never known a kidnapping case to end without a betrayal. Usually the betrayals surfaced while Rafe was probing the victim's life: extramarital affairs and secret vices were revealed. Too bad he didn't have better news for Mackinley. She was tough, though, and he had no doubt she'd be totally ruthless once she understood the truth. After all, she'd infiltrated Ransom High Risk, ripped off Rafe's database, and despite their nights together, the incident at the West Fourth Street station proved she still wasn't particularly swayed by Rafe's opinion. "Mackinley's made of strong stuff," he found himself saying, possessive pride making its way into his voice. "She's nobody's victim."

"Don't let your feelings get in the way, Rafe. We never sleep with clients for good reason."

Rafe let Shark's moralizing pass. Mackinley had never been a client in the usual sense. She'd become so much more. So had Barbara and K.G. "Given your wardrobe problems," said Rafe, "I figure you've got enough on your mind, so this is no time to start worrying about me."

Shark nodded grimly. "I hope not, Rafe. Have you decided what you want to do about Spain?"

"As soon as we get home, I'll talk to Mackinley. She has a right to be the first to know."

MACKINLEY BACKED RAFE against the closed door of
the bedroom, and he managed a smile, his hands rubbing down her hips, smoothing her tan wool skirt.
Tilting her head upward, she returned the smile, and
in the darkening winter twilight spilling through the
curtains the golden brown irises of her eyes looked
deeper amber, almost black. "Rafe..." Her voice
caught. "I want to thank you again. I know you're still
mad about what happened at the station, but—"

He pressed a finger to her lips.

She took another tack. "With you here, Mom and I
have felt so much better."

"Good." But after Spain was picked up, Rafe would
be leaving. Damn if he didn't want to stay, though.
He'd gotten used to this room, used to the too-narrow
bed they shared. His lips parted to tell her, but he
couldn't find the words. It was too bad Barbara had
gone to the store with K.G. Even though Rafe intended
to share the bad news about Spain privately, he
thought Mackinley's mom should be in the apartment.
The women had supported each other through the ordeal and now they needed to discuss it together.

Rafe pulled Mackinley closer, his voice dropped
and his words spun out like a thread of silk. "I wanted
you all day. I can't look at you without wanting you."

"Then have me."

"That easy, huh?"

"Should I fight?"

"No, I like you submissive."

"Then I'll fight like a hellcat."

"You won't let me win?"

"No, but go ahead and try, Rafe."

Despite the need to tell her about Spain, her soft vanilla scent had him lowering his head and using his five o'clock shadow to lightly abrade her neck. The kiss that followed was the wet, devouring kind that hungrily ate at her compliant lips. Her expectant shiver pushed licks of fire through his limbs, and his thighs tensed with a rush of potent need. "C'mon," he protested, since he knew this would quickly reach the point of no return. "I just want to talk to you." The second her mom returned, Rafe had to tell Mackinley about Spain.

"Mom took K.G. to the store with her," Mackinley coaxed. "And we've got a few minutes..."

The playful crawl of her bandaged fingertips up his shirtfront was even more convincing than her words, and as she loosened his tie and fumbled with the top buttons of his shirt, the rhythmic brush of her belly against his hardening sex made his breath quicken. "Did the big boss have a hard day at the office?" she purred.

Insatiable hunger stole his smile as he kissed her again, his lips moving on hers, exploring her mouth. He knew the soft curve of her belly by heart, and on the growing swell he pressed against it, he could feel tremors leaping beneath her skin. She needed him as much as he needed her, but Rafe feared things would change when Spain was behind bars and Rafe wasn't living here anymore. He braced himself. She'd seduced him so he'd help her, and they'd made a deal, right? Maybe that was what this meant to her. "A very rough day at work," he found himself murmuring.

"Because of your awful assistant, no doubt," Mackinley commiserated huskily. "You know, the one who keeps removing your clothes?"

Splaying a hand at the small of her back, Rafe guided her to where he felt most afflicted. "She's difficult to deal with," he admitted. "But a man's gotta do what a man's gotta do." Even though he needed her more than life, he thought of Spain again, and forced himself to draw back. "C'mon, why don't we start dinner before your mom gets back?"

"Men," Mackinley sighed loftily, oblivious to his inner turmoil. "All you ever want to do is talk."

He couldn't stop the slow grin that stretched his lips. "By now, you know better than that, Mackinley."

Her gaze was steady. "I have some firsthand knowledge."

"Secondhand, too," he returned, since he'd told her so much about his life.

"Are you sure you want to start dinner?"

He enjoyed her playful resistance. "Toying with me?"

"Should I be toying with somebody else?"

Rafe's lust-darkened green eyes glinted jealously at the thought. Suddenly, feeling powerless to fight her, he grasped the end of his tie, yanked it from his collar and tossed it aside. "You'd better not."

"No?"

"I seriously wouldn't recommend it."

She offered another lofty sigh. "What would you do to him?"

"Damn if I wouldn't kill him."

Her cheeks flushed at the promise. The pulse visibly racing in her throat, she reached under her skirt and slowly drew down her tights, stripping them off, and he watched shadows play on her golden hair as she stood again, straightening her shoulders. He let her finish unbuttoning his shirt, his throat going dry as she thrust fingers into his chest hairs. As she swirled the dark wild curls, her jagged nails snagged on his skin, scraping in a way that shouldn't have been stimulating, but was. "I'll understand if you're not up to it," she taunted.

He raised a hand and used his knuckles to gently trace her jaw. "I guess we'll never know. You've already pushed me too far, Mackinley." With a vengeful claiming, he took full possession of her mouth, establishing his mastery. He'd wanted this all day, and only after she softened and yielded did he cup her chin and gentle the pressure of their kiss. Grazing his thumb downward, he slowly stroked her neck as his tongue soothed her mouth. Groaning satisfaction, he pulled at her lips, suckling before plunging deeper once more. After a long moment he leaned back, his voice hoarse, the words heartfelt, "Damn if you don't drive me crazy, Mackinley Leigh."

Her mouth was swollen, red and damp; her brown eyes glazed and warm, the color of hot, tasty things that drizzled, like butter on browning biscuits. Her voice suddenly caught. "What's wrong?"

"You're too much woman for me, that's what." Rafe's husky voice was filled with amazement, and his appreciative eyes flicked over her face right before his mouth found hers again. Aching with need, too aware of the constricting confines of his clothes, he lowered his open-fingered hands, smoothing them from her back to her bottom, and he felt himself start to slip over the edge. Dragging her to him with sudden force, he inhaled sharply, drawing in her sweet female scent as she writhed against him. "I mean it when I say no woman's ever done this to me," he whispered.

"Then maybe you should play it safe and stop."

There it was again, that female taunt he couldn't resist. Instinctively, she knew how to bind him to her. "Damn if I'll stop," he growled. He couldn't anymore than she could. Not now, not ever. Night after night, he'd loved her. Enveloped in the inky darkness, he'd explored her as he had no other woman. Until dawn, he'd studied her with his hands and let his mouth wetly pleasure each unseen bare inch of her...until he was fastening his lips to her intimately, and she turned mindless and feverish under the heavy winter covers. All night she'd cling to his shoulders while he pressed his hand to her mouth, urging her to suck his thumbs and fingers, anything to muffle sounds that might wake Barbara or the baby.

For weeks, he'd only loved her in the dark.

"I want to see you," he said raggedly before kissing her once more. "Every inch." His eyes craved all the sights—the shimmer of dampness on her skin, the sweet contortion of her mouth as her pleasure built, the fretful, wild twists and turns of her hips, and how her eyes darted as her head tossed from side to side on the pillow—all as if Rafe would actually let her escape the maddening, building pressure he meant to give her now. Again. Drawing back, he traced his tongue over her teeth, then licked her lips, savoring their flavor. "And I want to hear you, too."

"Hear me?"

"Every sob you stifle in the night, Mackinley." His hand found hers, closed over it, and he brought it between his legs, wrapping her fingers around where he was so hard he could burst. His words roughened with need, "Let's go to bed."

"I'll lead," she whispered simply. "You follow."

"After you." He almost exploded when her hands caressed his aroused length first. Her fingers were too small to fully close around him but the immeasurably warm pressure sent his every last sense skyrocketing. Shuddering, he moaned and arched as the hot touch lowered, kneading where he was softer, fleshier.

Going out of his mind, he undid her blouse, his breath catching as he flicked open the front clasp of her bra, then pushed aside the cups. In his broad, dark hands, her full breasts felt wonderful, and he lifted them, his mouth settling with familiar greed. She tasted spicy today, peppery, and as he traced his tongue around and around a stiffened peak, his only coherent thought was that he and Mackinley deserved this last moment together before all hell broke loose; he'd give her every last ounce of pleasure before she realized she'd been miserably betrayed by a bastard who'd never deserved her. Sponging both her breasts now with the pad of his tongue, he waited until she was shamelessly hot, then he simply folded her in his arms, hoarsely growling, "You'll never know what you do to me."

"I think I do." She shivered with want. He felt her hands on him again, wrestling with his fly and unzipping his pants. He bit down hard on his lower lip, biting back a cry, only to have it torn from him when she reached inside his briefs; one soft excruciating finger brushed the bared head of his erection, tracing a drop of moisture.

"Everything about you's torture," he whispered.

He wanted all of her: her looks, her brains, her passion, the way she kept her sense of humor in the face of adversity. He backed her to the bed, and as she scooted onto it, he coaxed her onto her belly. She looked amazing lying on top of the covers, her elbows crooked, her hands sliding under a pillow.

He didn't bother removing his shirt. He kicked away his pants and briefs, his eyes roving from her hair, down her long neck, to the curving dip of her back, then to the rounded swell of her bottom under the prim skirt. With a throaty rumble, he kneeled between her legs, using both hands to push up the skirt, exposing white panties.

When she tried to turn to face him, he stayed her. "Don't move, sweetheart. I'm enjoying this too much."

"Me, too," she whispered.

With a shaky breath, he pulled the panties to her thighs and palmed the taut, quivering pale flesh of her bottom. Shuddering, he traced a finger where she was wet and open for him, making her cry his name, just the way he wanted. Carefully peeling her panties the rest of the way down, he raggedly said, "Damn if I don't like looking at you this way."

And then he leaned forward, catching her sharp, tangy scent, and felt something swift and wrenching inside him, a new fierceness he'd never experienced that he thought might be love. Bending lower, kissing and nipping, he flattened a hand and slid it between her and the mattress, gently lifting her a fraction.

"That's right." His lust-glazed eyes settled on her pale moist folds. "Let me see everything, Mackinley." Snagging his fingers in her moist, downy curls, he felt the heat emanating from her and was stunned by the dark, huge look of his own hands as he slowly, lovingly inserted a finger. Ignoring the resistant tightness, he pushed in another, two together now, until her soft gasps sent rippling shivers through his whole body.

"Let me..." His throat was suddenly dry, the strained words trailing off because there was no end to the things Rafe wanted to do with her. "Too much woman," he whispered again, his body burning now, his heart swelling as he watched her heave to meet his touch, her climax palpable—a scent, a sound, a breath. So very close.

He was sore with the need to be inside her now. Wordlessly withdrawing his fingers, not breaking the rhythm, he flung back his head, the tendons of his neck straining as he swiftly entered her, and she cried out with surprise, her throbbing, unsuspecting flesh closing around him as he surged, unsheathed and hard and yet as soft as pure velvet. Awash with emotion, he swelled inside her, so hot he thought he'd incinerate, so hard he thought he'd break. His eyes halfshut in ecstacy, he watched her move to meet his thrusts as he stroked the silken curve of her belly, then reached lower...lower. One vibrating touch to the slick bud—and she gushed, filling him with the pleasure of what he was giving. He came immediately, spilling into her, calling her name, then he buried his lips deep in her hair, kissing the strands as he urged her to face him, their joined bodies never separating. "I came inside you," he whispered in hoarse apology.

She swallowed hard, her hands under the shirt he

was still wearing, gliding down his naked back. "I don't care. I really don't. I'm glad."

He was, too. "You mean that, Mackinley?"

"I most certainly do," she whispered tremulously. "It feels so good."

Pressing his lips to the top of her head again, he wanted to tell her that she looked cute as hell right now, with her short hair mussed and a faint sheen of perspiration on her shoulders and her eyes glossy with satisfaction. Instead, because he'd registered the fact that a minute ago, he'd heard the front door open, he said, "We'd better get dressed."

"I know. I think Mom's back."

"She is. I heard her."

The next few minutes were a flurry of movement— her thrusting his trousers at him, him draping her tights over her shoulder. As he dressed, he willed his heartbeat to leave the danger zone, and then he said, "Before we go out there, there's something I have to say."

She glanced up, smoothing her skirt and frowning. "What?"

"I found your ex-husband."

THE WORDS STAGGERED Mackinley. For the first few minutes, she simply stood at the foot of the bed, listening carefully to Rafe and squinting in concentration, so she wouldn't miss anything important, but she still felt as if a heavy blanket had been thrown over her mental faculties. Finally, she said, "My husband's where?"

"*Ex*-husband."

"Sorry," she managed, wringing her hands. "I

know I keep saying that, but I've never called him my ex, probably because, well, I...I believe you only get married once. I believe so much in marriage. Deep down, I guess I still believe I...did something wrong."

"You didn't." Rafe draped an arm along the rail of the crib, his fingers curling around it, almost as if to stop himself from crossing the room. "You don't want me to pick him up?"

She inhaled sharply. "You mean call the cops?"

"Yeah."

"Rafe, Oliver wouldn't do this. My marriage might have failed—" She fought to keep the righteous indignation from her voice. "But I know Oliver. He must have been forced. Maybe somebody threatened me or the baby. He...he'd never do something like this. But...you say he's in Long Island? You're sure?" Now she felt like a parrot. "Long Island, New York?"

Rafe didn't look the least bit surprised by her reaction. She guessed he'd had plenty of time to anticipate it. He'd suspected Oliver, but he hadn't told her.

"Yes," Rafe said calmly. "Long Island, New York."

She realized her hand had crept up to the collar of her blouse, and now she mindlessly finished buttoning it. Her heart was palpitating; indignation mingled with feelings of betrayal. She was aware her skin was still warm, but her and Rafe's lovemaking now seemed a lifetime ago. "What about the Polaroid?" she forced herself to ask. "Oliver was posing with newspapers, so obviously he was in South America."

Rafe's lips set grimly. "I'm sorry, Mackinley. There's no mistake. He's been in the U.S. the whole time." Rafe offered the address, then lifted his hand from the crib rail and ran it through his dark hair distractedly. "I started to tell you when we got home, but I thought you'd want your mother…"

"What I want is the truth." Her stomach felt jittery and her heart was racing. *Rafe must think I'm such a fool.* "How long have you suspected this?"

Instead of answering, Rafe eyed her for a moment, then strode across the room and stopped in front of her. Resting both hands firmly on her shoulders, he stared deeply into her eyes. "Please remember—" his words carried a soft warning "—you're mad at Oliver, not me."

Wrong. Her knees felt weak. "Just answer the question."

His fingers molded more firmly around her shoulders. "I've considered the possibility ever since I saw the Polaroids. To be honest, it's unusual for a victim to keep his glasses intact."

Her lips parted in silent protest. "You should have been honest long before now. You mean to say you thought my husband was…" She could barely say it. "…was *stealing* from me? And you didn't even *tell* me?"

"Ex-husband. And I only suspected."

"Why? Do I look like the kind of person who can be so easily used? Do I look like a target?"

"You're the victim. That means you didn't do anything wrong. I've seen this a million times."

I'll bet. "So, that's why you said I was too trusting and gullible." To Rafe, she was probably only another statistic. "Am I the only victim you've comforted? Or was Charmaine…" She paused. Had Rafe just felt sorry for her?

"I helped Charmaine's brother," he said, "but this is

different and you know it. I began suspecting Oliver because, when there's so much money at stake, there are usually more kidnappers involved. A print on the Polaroid matches one I lifted from a handball racquet of his, too, and there are enough common points for an I.D. that will hold up in court."

She tried not to think of all the nights she'd prayed for Oliver, stifling tears and worrying if he was clothed and fed...and now she was supposed to send him to jail?

"He's probably been picking up the drop money, himself," Rafe added gently.

Her voice sounded panicky to her own ears. "Or you're making this up. You've never really wanted to help me find him. Maybe you're jealous."

Rafe's eyes turned watchful. "I haven't betrayed you, sweetheart," he said, anger lacing through the words. "You're embarrassed because you think you should have known the truth. You think you should have seen some clue."

She made a small choking sound. "Guess I'm a text-book case, huh, Rafe?"

"I've been in this business a long time."

Mackinley was convinced Rafe had to be mistaken. Her marriage hadn't been perfect, but she wasn't completely stupid. Oliver's parents had died when he was in high school, but he was from a good family. "He's...self-made. Determined. So...good-looking, well-educated, eager to provide. He was, he *is*, everything a man's supposed to be."

Rafe's green eyes darkened like a deep part of the ocean. "Thanks," he ground out.

"That's not what I mean," she cried. But even if she

had misjudged Oliver, how could she accept that Rafe Ransom was witnessing her humiliation? Even if Rafe wanted more from their relationship, how could she move on without understanding a past mistake of such magnitude?

Rafe squeezed her shoulders once more, the warmth of those huge hands seeping through her blouse, then he turned on his heel, found a briefcase, pulled out a folder and handed it to her. "If you don't believe me," he said, his voice controlled, "you'll find everything you need here."

Everything I need? Such as a loyal man? Huh, Rafe? Will I find that in your neat little folder?

"It's all here in black and white."

She forced herself to look, tears filling her eyes and making the small print blur. Slowly turning the pages, she saw the lab reports, the fingerprint analysis. There was a picture of Oliver outside a brick house with an address written at the bottom. And yet, even as she recalled how carefully she'd treated the Polaroid, how she'd slipped each into a sandwich bag, holding the edges with tweezers the way she'd seen on police shows, she was still certain Rafe had to be wrong.

Oliver couldn't really have respected her so little that he'd methodically stolen the fortune it had taken her dad years of backbreaking work to build. She couldn't see straight to read, and when she was done she definitely didn't want to look into Rafe's waiting eyes. She'd come to need him so much. Since he'd moved in, a comfortable domesticity had characterized their relationship, the very thing she'd once dreamed of sharing with Oliver. But Rafe wasn't the marrying kind, and while he enjoyed their lovemaking, he'd never indicated he wanted more. "I guess we know what everything means now."

Rafe stared at her. "Meaning?"

"You were supposedly helping me, but you didn't even involve me. Rafe, I don't know what's happened, but Oliver's honest. He was my husband. I should have known about this information, since it directly affects me and my family...his son."

Rafe's body was poised and tense. "Your family. I see."

She could barely go on and felt her throat closing. "I'm sorry," she said shakily. "This isn't what I expected at all."

Barely concealed anger made Rafe's green eyes glitter. "No, it's not, is it?" he demanded, his voice low. "It seems you were hoping I'd turn up some Latin American thug, the way they do on all the cop shows. Maybe you were anticipating Oliver's homecoming, thinking he'd be so grateful to you for saving him that he'd want to live happily ever after. Isn't that right?"

Maybe. Before you came into my life. Her heart missed a beat. "No. But there is a reasonable explanation. Someone forced Oliver, then took off with the money. Maybe afterward, he was afraid to face me, which is why he's living in that house on Long Island." She studied Rafe. "How could you suspect something like this and not tell me?"

"I'm not the bad guy. I was protecting you, sweetheart."

"I'm not a little girl," she bit out. "So don't patronize me." Suddenly furious, she tossed the file onto the still-rumpled bed, then she grabbed her coat and shrugged into it.

Rafe's voice was deceptively calm. "Where are you going?"

"To talk to Oliver."

"What?" he exploded.

She glared at him. "What do you expect me to do?"

"Call the cops."

But Oliver couldn't have put her and her mom through these months of unrelieved stress. Recalling their small private wedding ceremony and how her parents had flown from New York to Boston on short notice, she felt her heart squeeze. Her mom had been upset because it wasn't a big church wedding, but they'd wanted to rush, since Carter was sick. Now her heart ached when she thought of how she and her mother had sold the family's brownstone on Jane Street, and of how she'd transferred the money to a South American bank.

Into Oliver's hot little hands.

"Impossible," she murmured.

Rafe gripped the lapels of her coat, trying to slip it from her shoulders. "I know this is hard. But you've got to do the right thing now."

She glared at Rafe. "I just need to talk to him."

Rafe's eyes hardened. "He's pulled a con. He's going to jail."

"There's more to this," she said frantically, her mind flooding with images: of the tea-length dress and pearls she'd worn on her wedding day, of the organist who'd played her father's favorite Mozart piece. As she'd said, "I do," she'd nervously dropped her bouquet of pink roses, and Oliver had stooped lithely in his tux to retrieve it. Was everything in her life a lie? Was love an illusion? Was her mother sugarcoating the truth about her relationship with Mackinley's dad? "This can't be true," she said hoarsely, her throat raw. "Don't you understand? Haven't you ever believed in marriage? Rafe...you've never settled down. You told me you've never loved anybody enough to commit."

He looked positively dangerous. "I haven't?"

She knew she was hurting him; she was hurting herself because she cared so much for Rafe—she knew that now—but it was time to face facts. "That's what you said. And I know how you feel about charity cases. I found that out early on, so I appreciate your help."

"That's me. Mr. Magnanimous."

"I know Oliver will help us get the money back from whoever really took it," she managed, "so maybe I can..."

Rafe's lowered voice was scarcely audible. "Pay me?" Before she could respond, he leaned over the bed and lifted the folder. "Forget about it, sweetheart. That's what you can do." Snagging his coat, he shrugged into it and walked out of the bedroom. And then he looked back once—just long enough to very, very silently close the door behind him.

9

YOU'VE NEVER SETTLED down. You've never loved a woman enough to commit.

Maybe not until now.

Last night, Rafe had stood outside Mackinley's apartment clutching his duffel, cruel bitter wind blowing open his coat. So this was what he got for playing the Good Samaritan? he'd thought. Fuming, he'd stood there on the curb—exactly as he'd stood on curbs all over the world when it was time to go home—suddenly feeling as though the woman and her baby had ripped out his ever-loving heart.

Mackinley's sweet little mom had done a real number on him, too, Rafe thought now, squinting through the woods toward where Mackinley was parked in front of Spain's house. Barbara had cooked Rafe's favorite meals and ironed his shirts, and for the first time in his life he'd felt as if he had a mother. After Charmaine, he should have known better than to get emotionally involved.

After offering Barbara a gruff goodbye last night, he'd made the tactical error of smoothing a hand over K.G.'s head before heading for the door. "See ya, kid," he'd said.

The words had broken his heart, which was why he'd sat outside Mackinley's apartment all night long, not sleeping, intending to keep an eye on her when she headed for Spain's place, but then she hadn't left until this morning. No way was Rafe going to stand by and see Mackinley throw her life away on such a scumbag. Rafe was going to nail the jerk to the wall, which was why he'd asked Shark to follow him here, for backup.

"What's she doing in her car?" Rafe grumbled, feeling sleepless and grimy. "Gnawing her fingernails?" He couldn't see the front of the house from where he was, but he knew what it looked like: the two-story brick structure with a sharply pitched roof had built-in love seats on the front porch—exactly the kind of place he'd imagined sharing with Mackinley. In the driveway, Spain's compact car was packed to the gills, as if he was planning on taking a very long trip sometime soon.

Rafe couldn't wait to inform him the trip was to jail. *What are you waiting for, Mackinley? Get out and knock.* Had she changed her mind? Since she hadn't come here last night, Rafe guessed she'd had second thoughts about confronting Oliver.

Shoving his hands into his coat pockets for warmth, his heart suddenly squeezed. In one pocket was the gun Shark had brought him, but now Rafe realized G.G. was in the other. Pulling her out, he stared down at the long, tangled brown hair. Yesterday, K.G. had gotten tired of playing with her, so Rafe had put her into his pocket. Leaning over the passenger seat, he now laid her gently in the glove compartment. No doubt K.G. was going crazy without his girlfriend.

Rafe knew the feeling. He grazed his fingers over the comforting cold steel of the gun. Well, with any luck he'd find a good excuse to shoot Spain. Of course, Rafe would probably lose his toes to frostbite first. Hunching his shoulders to ward off the chill, he wondered if he should have waited beside the sliding glass doors that opened onto Spain's back patio, but Rafe figured he'd be warmer here. Now snowflakes were clinging to the windshield, cutting visibility. Glancing over the white powder dusting the ground, Rafe raised his eyes to Spain's unassuming, isolated hideout at the end of the cul de sac; it was nearly surrounded by woods.

At least the man probably wasn't too dangerous.

No, he was everything a man should be, as Mackinley had put it. Well, let her have her blond, blue-eyed banker husband, who looked so smart in those scholarly wire-rims. She could pretend all she wanted, but Spain hadn't even been violently snatched; he'd calmly flown himself from South America to New York, probably sipping martinis. Rafe imagined Spain happily driving himself to this brick house on Long Island, humming show tunes.

"Thank you, Miss Mackinley," Rafe suddenly said, as she finally emerged from her car. "The way you've been dawdling, you'd think I've got all day." He opened the car door, braced himself against the wind and stepped outside, leaving the door cracked, to avoid the noise of shutting it. Mackinley was wearing a red, waist-length jacket he could see easily as he flitted through the trees.

He just wished his dress shoes would stop crunching on the frozen ground as he slipped through the woods, and that he wasn't wearing yesterday's suit. When he paused, resting his back against a leaf-bare sycamore, he became aware of the birds' whistles and the animals scurrying through the underbrush. After a moment, he crept toward the house again.

Why, he was doing this, he didn't know. Mackinley sure didn't care a rat's behind about him. Now it was *her* baby, *her* family, *her* husband. As he slowly advanced toward where the woods and side yard met, Rafe tried to put himself in her shoes, but he knew he'd never talk to his ex-wife again if she'd done something as underhanded as what Spain had done.

Not if you'd had a baby together?

Maybe that would soften him, Rafe admitted. Maybe he'd have powerful feelings of denial. And this *was* in line with Mackinley's character, which included nerves of steel. Her need to handle things by herself had made her able to shoulder this burden and infiltrate Ransom High Risk. Rafe just wished she'd wanted something more from him. He hated being just another professional tough guy she'd needed to help her find Spain.

Suddenly, he saw Mackinley pause on the sidewalk. Hugging the baby tightly, she tensed and glanced around. "When it comes to realizing you're being followed, you've got good instincts, sweetheart," Rafe whispered. "I'll give you that." When it came to men, her instincts sucked.

Now Rafe glanced toward the main road, hoping Shark hadn't fallen asleep in the Humvee, then he turned his attention to Mackinley once more. Seeing the baby, he uttered a soft curse. No doubt, Mackinley felt Spain had a right to see his child, but Spain was a crook. And Rafe could never forgive her skewed sense of loyalty. When she started walking again, his eyes skimmed down the red jacket to where snug jeans hugged her tush, and he felt an unwanted rush of longing, followed by murderous male possessiveness.

"Oh, yeah," he muttered. "I can see you're really thinking with your mind now, Rafe."

Taking a deep breath, he bolted toward the backyard and patio, losing sight of Mackinley. Unused lawn furniture was stacked against the back of the house and Rafe's eyes settled on a glass of water Spain had left on a table; it was frozen solid. Tiptoeing to the sliding glass doors, Rafe tested them and was pleasantly surprised to find them unlocked. The curtains were open, too, so he could see into the den, then beyond that, into the living room.

But where was Mackinley?

It was taking her too long. Had she run back to the car for something? Had she changed her mind? Rafe tensed, waiting. Any second, he'd hear the muted sound of the doorbell. He imagined Mackinley standing on the front porch holding K.G., her heart pounding. Somewhere inside, Spain would tilt his head toward the sound, run downstairs and put his eye to the front door's peephole. Would he open the door?

Dammit, where was she? Rafe might be a hotshot hostage negotiator, but when it came to this particular woman and child, things were one-hundred percent nonnegotiable. Rafe hadn't come to talk. His hand closed over the gun. He'd come for action.

"I DON'T KNOW about this," Mackinley whispered, pausing on the sidewalk. She'd sat here a long time, sure Oliver was alone inside. The compact car parked in the driveway was packed with belongings that had to be Oliver's. She'd seen a handball racquet of the sort he liked to use, plain black suitcases of the sort he carried, and bottles of Evian water, which he always drank.

She returned to her car, got in, slammed the door and stared at the house, hugging K.G.. Her heart hammering, her eyes took in the woods surrounding the property, then the bare patches of frozen earth lining a long brick walkway. She guessed flowers were usually planted there in the summer.

Brushing her lips on K.G.'s forehead, she dug in her pocketbook for the phone. Flipping it open, she tried Rafe's apartment. "C'mon," she whispered. "Where are you, Rafe?" When there was no answer, she tried the Humvee.

Before the first ring, it was picked up. "Yeah, I'm here."

But it wasn't Rafe. "Shark?"

"Mackinley?"

Turning K.G. around in her lap, so he could play with the steering wheel, she said, "It's me."

"Where are you?" Shark said impatiently. "Are you still outside Spain's house or what?"

Her eyes darted to the house. "Yes. How did you know?"

"Don't worry about that now! Just get inside!"

Get inside? "What are you talking about? Where's Rafe?"

"Waiting for you to go inside."

"But I'm not," she protested, her eyes searching the yard for any sign of Rafe. "I thought about it all last night...and, well, anyway, I've got the baby with me.

Mom went to work, and it's Saturday, so there's no day care—"

"Mackinley," Shark interjected impatiently. "Just go. You're covered. And your ex is a con man. He's not dangerous, but we need you to help us catch him."

Her heart beat double-time. She'd lain awake all night, working through her denial, but she still couldn't quite believe how completely she'd been betrayed. "You're sure?"

"Get in there," Shark repeated urgently. "Before your ex sees you and makes a run for it. We can't afford to lose him."

She didn't want that to happen. Besides, a part of her still relished the opportunity to confront him. Her heart beating out of control now, she said, "Are you sure?"

"Yes. Go. Now."

Shark was clearly in no mood to talk. "Okay." Hanging up the phone, she whispered, "Here goes nothing."

"I'M SO GLAD you're here!" Oliver said.

Mackinley merely gaped as he stepped onto the porch and pulled her and the baby into his arms. He glanced down at the scant place he'd left between them. "And this is...?"

"Our son." Because she felt she'd betrayed Rafe with the words, she quickly added the nickname he'd given, "K.G."

Oliver's blue eyes misted with tears that made pure fury coil inside Mackinley. "A boy," he whispered, his voice strangled with unexpected emotion. She'd been prepared for anything at all—except an effusive welcome. She glanced around, half-expecting to see Rafe, then panicked as Oliver pulled her toward the threshold, saying in a hushed, conspiratorial tone, "Please...please. Come in. Both of you."

She stared at him. If he'd been stealing, would he hole up in a house so unassuming? she suddenly wondered. Wouldn't he be living more lavishly? His style of dress was the same, too, and he hadn't grown a beard, or switched to contact lenses in an effort to disguise himself. He looked cleaner than he had in the Polaroid, and he'd put on weight.

"Please," he repeated, rapidly gesturing. "Hurry."

"Why?" Glancing over her shoulder, she looked around the front yard, but there was still no sign of Rafe or Shark. And yet Shark had assured her they were here to help. She took another step inside.

"Just come in."

The place was cozy, well lit and warm, and scents of baking permeated the air, but Mackinley instinctively held K.G. closer, noting the circular layout of the interior. A living room to her right led to a kitchen, then to a den with sliding glass doors, and back to the living room again. Suddenly, she squinted. She could swear she'd seen a shadow pass the sliding glass doors. Was it Shark? Rafe? Relief flooded her.

"No one's here," Oliver assured her.

They most certainly are. "Looks like you're alone," she managed, taking in the new living room furniture and blue carpet.

"Don't worry, I can explain everything."

K.G. wiggled, sensing the tension, and Mackinley veered back just before his flailing fist clipped her jaw. "Shush," she whispered, bouncing him, but he started writhing. Mackinley didn't take her eyes from Oliver, though. He was acting almost as if he'd expected her; he'd probably seen her from a window before she knocked. That, or he was a good con man and used to lying.

But where was Rafe? Just thinking of him, Mackinley could feel his hands, his mouth, and hear his fervent whispers in the dark; she'd never shared anything like that with Oliver. On closer inspection, she decided there was something false about the way Oliver was looking at her. His eyes were too bright, his smile too broad. "Whose house is this?"

"As I said, I'll explain everything."

Any remaining denial was slipping away. "I'm waiting."

He gestured toward a straight-back chair near the door. "Please...sit."

She felt totally unnerved. "I'd prefer to stand."

"I understand," Oliver said smoothly. "But when you hear what I've been through, you'll realize nothing's as it seems."

"Oh, I'm starting to get the picture." And she wanted to know how she'd so misjudged this man. He'd pushed her away during her pregnancy, yes... but she'd never have guessed him capable of theft. She suppressed a shudder—and a flood of guilt. Could Rafe ever forgive her for wanting to come here? Last night she'd felt so conflicted....

"Please," Oliver said again, seating himself on a beige love seat. "Sit down."

Given how K.G. was squirming, she had no other choice but to perch on the edge of the chair near the door. The longer she stared at Oliver, the more everything felt unbalanced. Was this really a man she'd married? A man she'd feared dead? Somehow, she kept her voice calm. "I want to know why you stole a fortune my father spent a lifetime building."

"I don't know where to start. I've wanted to call so many times. You aren't going to believe any of it."

Probably not. She rocked K.G., hoping to calm him. At least his diaper wasn't wet. This definitely wasn't the time for a change. Her eyes darting around, she tried her best to get Oliver talking. "I was so sure something awful had happened to you." That much was true. Night after night, she'd been eaten up with guilt because she was in a warm bed while Oliver was suffering. "I thought you were being tortured. Or that you were dead."

Oliver, the consummate con man, was watching her carefully. "You look well."

Hysteria rose in her throat. "This is just like our marriage," she couldn't help but say. "I remember it now."

"Remember what?"

"How we talked a lot but never said anything."

And then everything happened in a flash. K.G. suddenly wrenched in her arms, nearly falling, but Oliver swept from the love seat and whisked the baby from her arms saying, "Watch out, little guy. Boy, Mackinley, he's a wiggler, isn't he?" Smiling, Oliver returned to the love seat, settled the baby in his lap and stared down lovingly—all in a heartbeat.

Mackinley had stood, a very bad feeling curling inside her. *Rafe. Where are you?* "Put him down, Oliver."

Oliver sent her a glance of censure. "I want to hold my son," he said silkily. "After all this time, is that too much to ask? So many bad things have happened...and now you want to withhold my son?"

It didn't help that K.G. was taking to Oliver as she once had—like a kitten to cream. On a surge of fear and humiliation, she took a step forward. "Give me the baby."

Oliver's eyes darted to the stairs behind her. "Take it easy, Mackinley," he whispered. "I was kidnapped. They let me answer the door. They told me to lure you inside."

Wrenching around, she stared upstairs. But no...no, Oliver was lying! She jerked her head back just in time to see him draw a pistol from his pocket.

"You were always so damn gullible, Mackinley."

She watched in horror as he rose from the love seat with K.G. "Please put him down, Oliver."

"Don't worry. I have no intention of harming my own flesh and blood. After you got pregnant, I lost interest. You were right about that. But I always wanted this baby. And now he's mine." Slowly, Oliver started backing towards the den, toward the sliding glass doors leading outside.

Her few weeks at Ransom High Risk had taught Mackinley that escalating emotions could be deadly in hostage situations, so she kept her voice calm. "I want to talk this out. But before we can do that, you need to put K.G. down."

"As if you care about anyone but yourself."

What did Oliver mean by that? "I care."

"Not when things went wrong for me at the bank."

Keep him talking. Silently, she cursed Rafe and Shark for taking their good old time. How K.G. was smiling up at his father was breaking her heart, too. She wasn't the only one who'd been sucked in by the man's considerable charms. "You always said work was fine, Oliver."

He took another step backward. "I was losing millions. That's why I had to make a fresh start."

She took a surreptitious step forward as he backed toward the den. "But Daddy was sick when we got married," she said, fighting another wave of anger. "Why didn't you stick around? I was about to inherit."

"This way I have all the money. No strings attached."

Terror coursed through her at the words. No wonder she hadn't seen his betrayal coming. Oliver was slick. Good-looking, smart, educated. But a con man, too, incapable of healthy emotions. The fact that he was voicing no guilt or concern made her heart pound out of control. She had to get K.G. back. Could she sprint through the kitchen, then into the den and catch Oliver from behind? "How could you do this?"

"Both you and your mother think every man can live up to the great Carter Leigh, the self-made millionaire," he snarled. "Well, guess who's the self-made millionaire now?"

Mackinley wanted to say he couldn't hold a candle to her father's legacy of hard work and human decency. Reaching the threshold to the den, Oliver waved the gun. "Do what I say and I won't hurt you."

"Put down my son and I'll do anything you want."

"You'll do it anyway. Toss your car keys on the floor in front of my feet."

Her body was growing warm as adrenaline

pumped, bringing a metallic taste to her mouth. "You're not taking my son."

"*My* son," corrected Oliver.

She shook her head. "How did I ever believe in you?" *Because some people really are good.* Her eye caught another flash of movement; Rafe was on the back porch, outside the sliding glass doors. He was in yesterday's clothes, so he must have sat in the Humvee all night, in the cold, waiting to follow her. A lump lodged in her throat. *He'd never have come here if he didn't love us.*

He moved fully into the line of her vision, his skin blue from the cold, the collar of his coat raised against the wind. She avoided looking at him so Oliver wouldn't realize someone was behind him. Motioning, Rafe indicated she should throw her keys toward Oliver.

"Fine," she said loudly, withdrawing them from her pocket. Jingling, they hit the carpet, and Oliver scooped them up and into a pocket. "But I wasn't going to follow you, Oliver," she continued, "all I want is K.G. Later, we can negotiate a joint agreement," she lied.

"No negotiation."

You've got that right, she thought as Rafe's hand curled around the door handle. His body was still as a statue, his steady green eyes riveted to Oliver's back. She thought of Rafe's strong, steely, corded forearms. Arms that had held her—and that were now about to capture their prey.

Oliver had backed far into the den. He was five feet from the sliding glass doors, then four, then three. Any second, Oliver was going to whirl around to open the doors and make a run for it, but he'd find himself face to face with Rafe Ransom.

"The police are coming," she ventured, stepping forward so she could rush Oliver from the front when it was time. "I called them, Oliver."

"You're lying."

Oliver paused, not knowing another man—a far more powerful man—was standing silent sentinel behind him. Staring at her, Oliver looked sad, and she glimpsed the man he'd been when she met him. Oh, he'd never have been like Rafe—self-made with nerves of steel and mastery in the bedroom. But Oliver had once possessed a heart.

"What happened to you?" she whispered.

"Life, that's what. But who cares? My luck's about to change."

"Afraid not," Mackinley whispered.

As Oliver took a final step backward, the door rolled open and a hand thrust out, grabbing him from behind. Another brought a gun to Oliver's cheek.

"Nice and easy," said Rafe. "I want you to put down that little package you're carrying."

Oliver's bravado vanished. "The gun?"

"That, too," returned Rafe. "But we'll start with K.G."

10

MACKINLEY RUSHED forward to rescue K.G. while Rafe subdued Oliver. A second later, Shark barreled through the front door, and she felt a blast of winter air. Whirring sirens screamed in the distance.

Shark called, "Rafe?"

"Back here. In the den."

Pressing a hand to her heart, Mackinley whirled around, feeling a surge of gratitude as Shark strode into the room. "Hey, Mackinley," he said as he helped Rafe finish making a citizen's arrest. "The cops are on their way. I called."

Rafe stepped back as soon as Oliver was handcuffed, but he avoided Mackinley's eyes. "Thanks, Shark. I hear the sirens."

"Rafe," Mackinley managed breathlessly as she continued stroking the precious soft curve of K.G.'s head. "Thanks for being here." Leaning forward, she pressed the baby into his arms, surprised to feel his hesitation. Hadn't Rafe followed them because he loved them?

Suddenly, Mackinley wasn't sure. Almost unwillingly, Rafe took K.G., his lips twisting grimly. He said, "Maybe there was something to the old man's sensitivity training, after all."

"Meaning?"

"Meaning someday, I'd like to be treated that way. I know that now."

She stared up into green eyes that were hot, as always, with male awareness. "What way?"

"The way you treat your...husband."

She could only stare. Hadn't Rafe guessed what she felt for him? "Ex-husband," she corrected, saying it for the first time. "Rafe, I don't love him. I felt obligated. I didn't want to believe he'd stolen from us...." Last night, she'd been shocked to see the evidence. "Before that, I felt it would help to talk to him. How can I move on..." *How can we move on, Rafe?* "...if I didn't know where I went wrong?"

Rafe didn't respond to that. "Maybe someday," he continued, "a woman'll turn a blind eye no matter what *I* do. I just hope, if it ever happens—" Rafe nodded toward the living room where Shark had taken Oliver to be processed by the arriving officers "—that I deserve it more than that guy."

She knew this might be her only chance to say what she felt. "It's already happened, Rafe. I'm in love with you."

Shrugging, Rafe stared down. His hooded eyes were filled with emotion as he brushed a gentle kiss to K.G.'s head, then with obvious reluctance returned the baby. Wordlessly, Rafe slipped through the sliding glass doors, then stopped. Reaching a long arm back inside, he rubbed his knuckles lightly down K.G.'s cheek, then down hers in a way she knew she'd feel for the rest of her life. His words would stay with her, too. "You love me?"

"Yes. I do."

"I don't think so, sweetheart."

Mackinley would have corrected him, but he was already gone.

"OH, DEAR!" Barbara's alarmed voice came from the hallway. "The movers will be here any minute. Have we found G.G.?"

K.G. bounced in his walker, chortling. "Ga-ga! Ga-ga!"

Mackinley stared through the curtainless bedroom window watching the snow flurries. "That's right. G.G.," she said, wishing Rafe would call.

When she glanced at him, K.G. grinned.

"Good boy. Give Mom a big smile." Lifting him, Mackinley glanced around at the stacked packing boxes, all of which were marked with red Ms, so the movers could differentiate them from the blue Bs, belonging to her mother. They were moving to separate apartments, but it was for the best; for the first time, both women were going to be on their own. When Mackinley's gaze landed on the stripped bed she'd shared with Rafe, she hugged K.G. more tightly.

"Mackinley," her mother called. "K.G. loves that doll."

"She's probably buried in one of the boxes, Mom. She'll resurrect when we unpack."

"Why don't you call Rafe? Just ask if he's seen her?"

Mackinley wished she had the nerve. Earlier today, she'd caught herself standing stock-still with her hand on the phone, but she'd refrained from picking it up. At least the flurry of moving kept her mind off Rafe. And anyway, what was there to think about? Apparently, he'd taken all the physical comfort he wanted, right? Hadn't he done exactly what he'd promised and found Oliver? Had she really been expecting something more?

Now life was peopled with banking officials and detectives. From behind bars, Oliver had shown his true colors, saying he wanted nothing to do with his son, and a prosecutor had assured Mackinley and Barbara that Oliver's long prison term wouldn't be conducive to parenting a child, anyway. Lightly pinching her son's nose, Mackinley thought of her confrontation with Oliver. That day, she'd realized K.G. needed a dad, but not his biological one.

He needs Rafe.

So did she.

But she was a two-time loser. First Oliver, now Rafe. And it was all her fault. She'd loved too much, and would have believed almost anything, except the truth. She'd most certainly learned her lesson. Lowering her head, Mackinley brushed her chin against the top of K.G.'s head to stop its sudden quivering. "We'll be fine, sweetheart."

Fortunately, Oliver had been lying low, so he hadn't yet spent the money from her father's estate, and retrieving it had allowed Mackinley to repurchase the building where she'd been living. Crews were replastering, painting and replacing the noisy pipes, and the tenants were thrilled. And she liked the new apartment she'd rented in the West Village, around the corner from where she'd grown up. It felt like years since she'd seen the local proprietors—Jacques the florist, Mr. Kim at the deli, and Chin-Lee at the Chinese laundry.

Not that she could go back home again. She couldn't be a child forever, and her mother was grow-

ing in new directions, too, settling into life without
Carter. Barbara was moving uptown, near her new job
at the Museum of History, and it seemed to be a job
she was destined to keep. *Difficult changes but neces-*
sary, Mackinley thought, and she was glad she and her
mother were making the slow transition to being adult
friends.

"Was that the buzzer, dear?"

"I'll answer it!" Mackinley dropped a smacking kiss
on K.G.'s forehead, grabbed his baseball cap and
snuggled it onto his head as she ran for the door. But it
wasn't Rafe. Her heart breaking, she buzzed in the
mailman, then swung open the door and waited.
"You've got a package?" she said when he appeared.

"Express Mail, ma'am." He thrust out a clipboard.
"Mind signing?"

As she scribbled, the mailman leaned to get a better
look at K.G. "Cute," he pronounced, tugging down
the bill of the baseball cap. "Yours?"

Mackinley managed a smile. "His name's K.G."
And she couldn't say it without thinking of Rafe.

She shut the door, then opened the package and
drew a sharp breath while K.G. went wild, flapping
his arms excitedly. "Here you go," she said. "Looks
like Rafe found G.G." After a moment, she added,
"He even dressed her. Sort of."

It really hurt that he hadn't used this excuse to visit.
Didn't he care at all? And how could he not, after all
they'd shared? At night she could still hear the strong
wild beat of his heart, and in the darkness she could
still see that savage sexual glint in his eyes. She often
imagined she was curling her fingers in his chest hairs,
and feeling his hands as they grazed patterns on her

thighs. Her fortune was recovered and justice was served, but Rafe had left her aching.

Yes, at the very least, he should have returned G.G. personally, Mackinley fumed, whirling around and heading for the dining room. Undoubtedly, free-and-easy Rafe Ransom figured he'd just done his duty, tying up the last thread of Oliver's case into a neat little knot.

Well, things weren't finished yet, not until Mackinley had the last word. K.G. was holding the doll by the ankles, and as he happily banged her against Mackinley's shoulder, Mackinley glanced down at the flying red hair and grimaced. Her temper rose as she took in the grass skirt, halter top and high heels. She'd bet Rafe had dressed G.G. that way just to annoy her. "What?" she muttered. "Was he afraid he'd be arrested for sending a naked woman through the U.S. mail?"

"Are the movers here?" called her mother in alarm.

"Just the mailman." Mackinley rifled through her pocketbook, bypassing more tear-stained wadded tissues than she wanted to count, in search of her checkbook.

She flipped it open. "Personally," she said to K.G., as she poised a pen over a check, "Rafe's overpriced." Her heart suddenly hammering, she belatedly admitted there were some things a fully awakened woman couldn't put a price on. Nevertheless, she calculated Rafe's fee, quickly wrote out the check, then addressed and stamped the envelope.

Just as she started to lick it, her heart lurched. Rafe had been so wrong. She was in love with him. She couldn't live without him. But she licked the envelope, anyway, the glue tasting so bitter that it brought tears to her eyes.

"SHE'S THE MOST annoying woman I've ever met," Rafe fumed, pacing around the conference room's round table. "Why would she send a *check?*"

"Women are strange," offered Jack helpfully. He stared ponderously down at the check on the table, then nervously toyed with the end of his red, white and blue tie. "But at least it's an opening bid, Rafe, and now we can start the negotiation."

"We should definitely let her sweat it out a few more days, the way we usually do," began Shark righteously, tugging at the cuffs of a maroon pin-striped suit jacket. "Meantime, I hate to bring this up, sir, but if Mackinley and Rafe aren't seeing each other anymore, can we quit wearing these stupid suits?"

Jack glared at Shark. "No!"

Rafe sent everyone a murderous glance. "Where does she get *off?*"

Shark sighed. "Obviously at the stop that says, 'Out of Rafe Ransom's life forever.'"

"So she sends me a check? As if I provided stud services?"

"Son," coached Jack, "this is a negotiation. Keep your emotions out of it."

"Right," said Shark. "This is like any other case, Rafe, except now it's your heart that's being held hostage."

"Let's not get overly dramatic," said Rafe grimly, even though he knew it was true. He'd gone to Spain's hideout, prepared to fight for Mackinley, but the fact that she'd gone there also, hoping to see Spain, had infuriated Rafe. Jealousy had blinded him.

"Anyway, Rafe," returned Shark, "I think you're looking at this the wrong way. I mean, I like Mackinley a lot. She's really grown on me. But you're experiencing a luxury problem here. After a breakup, most guys don't get checks, they only get bills and invoices."

"So true," Jack agreed heavily, his frown making the scars above his eyebrows draw together. "But, Shark, that's beside the point. What we need is to find a solution for Rafe and Mackinley now. A win-win."

"A win-win," Shark repeated uncertainly. "Maybe we should ask Silencer how he interprets her sending the check."

"Not Silencer." Rafe shoved his hands angrily in his pockets. "He's been divorced three times already."

"Magnum?" asked Shark.

"He's never even had a girlfriend. Women hate his gambling."

"Excellent point." Shark nodded. "We'd better leave them out of this strategy session."

Jack worriedly scratched his bald head. "Son," he finally said, "I think by sending this check, she's trying to tell you she no longer cares about her husband."

"*Ex*-husband," muttered Rafe. "Why can't anybody get that right?"

Shark considered. "Last time you saw her, you said she called him her ex for the first time, right? And she'd never done that before?"

"No," admitted Rafe. "It was a first."

Jack nodded slowly, contemplating the significance.

"Right before I proposed to Rose, I think she did something like this."

Rafe stared. "My mother sent you a *check*?"

"Son, you're not listening." Jack's lips thinned with temper. "Rose did something *similar*, but it wasn't exactly the same thing." Narrowing his dark, beady eyes and pressing a beefy fist to his mouth, Jack tried hard to remember more. Finally, he shook his head. "I can't remember. That woman had my head so turned around that nothing made sense..."

Rafe barely heard. He was staring down at the check again. Usually, Mackinley's letters were small and neat, just like Mackinley, but now she was writing in cursive, with looping flourishes. "It's like she thinks she's signing the Declaration of Independence."

Shark frowned. "Why not just tell her she's going to be free over your dead body?"

Jack pondered a long moment, then he shook his head. "Good tactical thinking, Shark, but Mackinley's a lady, and strong-arming might backfire." He sighed again. "K.G. sure was so cute, though, remember? It was nice to finally have a baby around again." Quickly, Jack added, "I didn't mean to invalidate you, Rafe. I'm glad you grew up."

Rafe held up a staying hand. "No need to explain, Dad," he said, trying not to think about how much he missed the baby himself, or to notice that his father's beady eyes were growing misty. Apparently, Jack had it all figured out. Rafe was supposed to marry Mackinley and be a father to K.G. They'd move to the burbs, and Rafe would quit traveling and run the New York office. Meantime, Jack could retire and join the syn-

ergy lecture circuit. "I really do miss that kid," Jack
said once more.

"Quit trying to make me feel guilty, Dad."

"Sorry," sighed Jack. "But Mackinley was so nice."

And naughty. Not a lonely night went by that Rafe
didn't battle warring feelings. No sooner would he
squelch his dark anger than he'd be burning up with
need, missing her. His eyes narrowed.

"I don't know what got into her," Shark continued,
shaking his head. "When she called while we were at
Spain's, waiting to infiltrate, she sounded like she really wanted to talk to you."

Rafe turned slowly and stared at Shark. "When she
called?"

Shark squinted. "Yeah. When she called the Humvee."

"She called the Humvee? Why didn't you tell me?"

Shark peered at Rafe a long minute, then shrugged.
"What was there to say? She called looking for you
and I said you were waiting for her to go inside."

Rafe's chest constricted. "She went in because she
knew I was there?"

Shark still didn't quite understand. "She was about
to go home. Said she'd changed her mind about talking to him. But I told her to go inside, Rafe. We'd been
waiting all night."

Rafe couldn't believe it. Staring down at the check
again, he saw the win-win. Which meant it was time to
negotiate.

"THE FLOWERS ARE beautiful, Jacques." Mackinley
parked K.G.'s stroller on the sidewalk in front of the

florist's shop. "But the daffodils are my favorite. I don't know why."

"Everybody says they're like fluted cups that have caught the day's sunshine, my darling."

"That must be it." Smiling, Mackinley tugged up the zipper of a tan jacket she was wearing over black leggings. "Roses," she murmured, glancing over the buckets of blossoms. "And you've got lilies... mums...tulips." Bright petals waved in the breeze, doing her heart good.

Not that it would last.

Late at night, when it was quiet, Mackinley was getting shameless. That's when she missed Rafe the most. Shutting her eyes, she'd let her fantasies run wild, pretending he was everything from a stableboy, to a dark, devilish lord of the manor. But no matter how Rafe appeared in her dreams, everything about him was merciless torture—his hot mouth, his sure tongue, the fire of his eyes. She dreamed both of soft whispers and dirty words spoken in the heat of passion until the dreams were so real that she could feel Rafe's warm breath against her skin and even feel him inside her, thrusting deep, burning and stretching her.

"Mackinley?"

"Yes?"

Oblivious to her thoughts, the rotund Frenchman gestured with his hand. "I am just glad it's unseasonably warm, so I could put the flowers outside."

"Unseasonably warm," she agreed, her mind still on Rafe. After another moment of chitchat, she said goodbye. "Nice to see you, Jacques."

"Nice to have you in the neighborhood again."

Saturday tourists crowded the streets, and the fresh

air was alive with spring's first false alarm. Tonight, cold temperatures would return, but right now yellow-green leaves were sprouting, visible on saplings planted in the sidewalks. As Mackinley tried to enter her building, she had to pause, so a couple could finish kissing in the doorway. Watching them made her heart ache again.

That kiss looks so good.

She was pushing open the apartment door, trying to forget the caring she'd seen in the couple's eyes, when she heard his voice. "Mackinley?"

The breath left her chest, and her eyes suddenly stung with tears she wasn't about to shed. Pushing the stroller across the threshold, she turned to face Rafe, and his eyes so totally captured hers that she barely noticed his threadbare jeans or bone-colored windbreaker, or that he needed a shave. "Well," she managed. "This is most certainly a surprise."

He tilted his head and slanted his luscious green eyes in mock censure. "It shouldn't be."

"No?"

"Sorry, sweetheart." Rafe came inside, kicking the door shut with a casual finality that made her heart race. "But you were a charity case."

She had no idea where he was headed with this, but she took a deep steadying breath; the beat of her heart remained wild, though, sending blood through her veins with the speed of fire tearing across sun-dry brush lands. "A charity?"

"Yeah. You know, like Save the Whales. Or the Animal Rescue League." Rafe nodded ponderously, sexily chewing his bottom lip. "But I've begun to think we need to negotiate a new arrangement now..."

She managed to match his tone. "Ah, an arrangement?"

His voice dropped with husky promise. "One where you work off your debt."

She nodded sagely, catching the handle of the stroller so she could pull it further inside the room. "I think you'll need to come all the way inside for that."

"If I must," said Rafe walking toward her.

"You must." As her hungry eyes drifted down his broad, strong chest, she noticed the bouquet of daffodils he clutched against his thigh, and her throat threatened to close with emotion. "You followed me from Jacques'?"

Rafe held out the flowers. "He said you liked these."

As she took them, her hand shook, giving away the feelings she could barely suppress. "Jacques says they're yellow because they've caught the sunshine," she said softly. And right now, she felt as if Rafe had given her sunshine itself.

"I say they're the color of your hair."

Her eyes settled solemnly on his, and her voice lowered. "I love them."

Rafe edged closer, gazing down at her. "What about me? Did you mean what you said?"

Oh, yes. I meant it all. "Which thing I said, Rafe?"

"That you love me?"

Feeling shaky, she reached out and clutched her free hand around the stroller handle for support. "Yes. And you were right," she continued quietly, "I was so totally wrong in going there...I mean, after you showed me all the evidence, I shouldn't even have considered going to Oliver's."

Rafe came closer, cupping her chin and bringing her gaze back to his. "You went inside because I was there. Shark told me." He paused. "And I'm still here, Mackinley." His voice lowered a notch. "Right here."

They stared at each other for a long moment.

A slight smile suddenly twisted her lips. "Hmm. Not so fast," she murmured. "I thought this was a negotiation."

He unzipped her jacket and slid his arms inside and circled them around her waist. His hands were still chilled from the air and felt cool on her hips, and his near proximity made it seem as if years had passed since they'd made love. He said, "I'm all for going slow."

She considered. "If I learned one thing, it's that I gave too much in my marriage. I could so easily have become the kind of wife my mother was...a woman behind the man."

Rafe tilted his head. "I thought you said they had the perfect marriage."

"I idealized it," Mackinley countered.

"But now you've come to your senses and want it all?" Rafe guessed, his bemused lips parting. Before she could respond, he nuzzled her cheek, and she'd never felt anything better than the rough scrape of his chin. He added, "Feel free to keep negotiating."

"First tell me what made you decide to come over."

"Synergy," he returned, the rumble of his voice warming her. "And the fact that I've missed you— you, your mom and K.G."

"So, now you want a win-win?"

"I'm hoping. I've fallen for you, Mackinley." He sighed, brushing a strand of hair from her forehead.

"Damn if I haven't." Pulling her closer, he captured her mouth, the first touch of his lips flooding her with need.

"No kisses," she chastised on a sigh. "This is business."

His voice turned invitingly rough. "Good thing I'm your boss."

She stared into his sparkling green eyes. "If you were...something more...would we move to the burbs?"

"Would you be willing to settle for a man who works nine to five and manages a business, so his retired father can travel?"

Her heart swelled. They'd never discussed it, but she'd never be able to accustom herself to long separations and his dangerous work. She pretended to consider. "So you'd be in the office all the time?"

He nodded.

After a long pause, she shook her head. "I have a few conditions."

His eyes narrowed. "I'm listening."

"I quit my job, work in publishing again and get to hire your next assistant."

Rafe sent her a mock frown. "Would that be from somewhere other than the Francesca agency?"

"Boy," said Mackinley with a soft chuckle. "You're swift. I'm thinking of Mrs. Alvarez. You know, from up on the fifth floor, in the old apartment building?"

Rafe's lips parted in protest. "The lady with the mustache?"

Mackinley nodded. "And don't be rude. She's efficient, bilingual and very unemployed."

Rafe didn't look too happy. "Only on one condition," he countered slowly.

Mackinley's eyes narrowed to slits. "Sorry. But Mrs. Alvarez is nonnegotiable."

Rafe blew out a lofty sigh. "You haven't even heard my terms yet."

Mackinley's frown deepened. "What do you want?"

"Another baby." Her breath caught as he continued, "And the promise, right now, that you'll marry me before next Valentine's Day, Mackinley."

She tried to smile, but she felt too shaken. Threading her fingers into his hair, lightly scraping her new nails against his scalp, she gazed at the big dark-haired hulking hunk of a man she'd grown to love.

"Your move now," he said, his expression softening when he saw the tears gathering in her eyes. "Will you marry me?"

Blinking rapidly, she somehow managed to stretch her lips into a smile. "Damn if I won't, Rafe," she whispered, her voice low with the emotion filling her heart, her mind racing with ideas about their future. As she gazed into his eyes, a strange calm suddenly settled over her, and that's when she knew how very right this was. "Are you satisfied now, Rafe?" she whispered huskily.

"Satisfied?" That wasn't even the word. This was exactly the win-win he'd been seeking, and in the breath before his lips found hers, Rafe raggedly whispered back, "Most certainly, Mackinley Leigh. Oh, most certainly."

If you enjoyed what you just read,
then we've got an offer you can't resist!

Take 2 bestselling love stories FREE!

Plus get a FREE surprise gift!

Come escape with Harlequin's new

Series Sampler

**Four great full-length Harlequin novels
bound together in one fabulous volume
and at an unbelievable price.**

Be transported back
in time with a
Harlequin Historical®
novel, get caught up
in a mystery with Intrigue®,
be tempted by a hot, sizzling romance
with Harlequin Temptation®,
or just enjoy a down-home
all-American read with
American Romance®.

You won't be able to put this collection down!

On sale February 2000 at your favorite retail outlet.

HARLEQUIN®

Temptation

When times are tough, and good men are hard to find... who are you going to call?

FANTASY FOR HIRE

Temptation #759 *CHRISTMAS FANTASY*
by Janelle Denison
On sale November 1999

Fulfilling women's fantasies was Austin McBride's business. But his gorgeous client, Teddy Spencer, had Austin doing some fantasizing of his own....

Temptation #767 *VALENTINE FANTASY*
by Jamie Denton
On sale January 2000

Reporter Cait Sullivan was determined to expose Fantasy for Hire, even if it meant going undercover. But once she met sexy-as-sin Jordan McBride, all she could think about was getting him "under the covers"...

Fantasy for Hire
Your pleasure is our business!

Available at your favorite retail outlet.

HARLEQUIN®
Makes any time special ™

Visit us at www.romance.net

HTFFH

COMING NEXT MONTH

#765 BILLY AND THE KID Kristine Rolofson
Bachelors & Babies

Everyone in Cowman's Corner, Montana, believed the baby left
on Will "Billy" Wilson's doorstep was his. And Will wasn't
saying otherwise. So when Daisy McGregor agreed to help him
look after "the kid," she knew she was risking her heart.
Because she was looking for a family kind of man—and Will
had *no* plans to be a daddy or a husband.

#766 MILLION DOLLAR VALENTINE Rita Clay Estrada

Mall exec Blake Wright really needed to loosen up. Who better to
help out than Crystal Tynan, masseuse and free spirit? Except
she seemed to rub him the wrong way...especially when she
started getting overly creative with the window dressing of her
aunt's flower shop. Still, there *was* a sizzling attraction...and it
was Valentine's Day.

#767 VALENTINE FANTASY Jamie Denton

Fantasy For Hire...*Your pleasure is our business!* Newspaper
reporter Cait Sullivan was determined to expose this unusual
company as a sham, even if it meant going undercover. But once
she met sexy-as-sin owner Jordan McBride, all she could think
about was getting him "under the covers"....

#768 BARING IT ALL Sandra Chastain
Sweet Talkin' Guys

Reporter Sunny Clary was on a mission—to disclose the true
identity of legendary male stripper Lord Sin. Only, every path
led her to sexy playboy Ryan Malone. But it was her reaction to
the two men that had her confused. Lord Sin made her yearn....
Ryan Malone made her burn.... How could she be drawn to such
completely different men? *Or were they so different?*

CNM0100

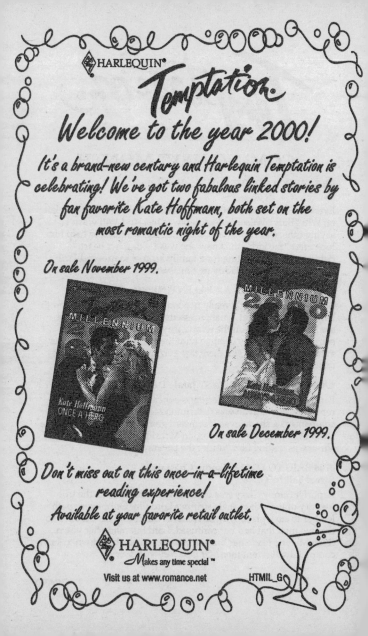